Sore Must Be The Storm

An Inkwells & Anvils Anthology

E. P. Fuselier   S. J. Delacosta   Caspar

Grace F. Hopkins   Ben Stapleton   Madeline Shepley

Augustin Cavalier   Catherine Broussard   Paige Guerra

Gwendalina K.K. Buller   Elizabeth Ruda

*In memory of Pope Francis,
who announced the Jubilee Year of Hope which inspired us to choose
this theme for our anthology.*

Requiescat In Pace

"Hope" is the thing with feathers -
That perches in the soul -
And sings the tune without the words -
And never stops - at all -

And sweetest - in the Gale - is heard -
*And **sore must be the storm -***
That could abash the little Bird
That kept so many warm -

I've heard it in the chillest land -
And on the strangest Sea -
Yet - never - in Extremity,
It asked a crumb - of me.

— Emily Dickinson

Contents

Foreword

HOPE is a difficult virtue to write about. On its surface, it can seem so fluffy, cheerful, even saccharine. But as soon as one starts to delve into what hope is—for ourselves and how we live it on a daily basis—that is where I find we uncover its more complex nature. I believe Dickinson captures this conundrum well when she describes it as *"the thing with feathers,"* a delicate creature that surely is subject to the whims of the wind. But in the same poem, she writes, *"Sore must be the storm that could abash the little bird."*

The stories you will find in this anthology are full of mighty storms of various kinds, all holding a power that should overcome a fragile thing with feathers. And yet, it is the storm who must be sore. Because hope's power, while not as showy, *"never stops at all."* Hope has a subtlety, an unspoken power that we can't grasp until we experience its grace.

As we put together this collection of stories, we discussed amongst ourselves how we personally imagined hope. For myself, it is a logic defying, bitter pebble that hurts to swallow but mysteriously keeps us alive. For another, it is a life preserver that allows us to stay afloat. For another, it is holding on with white knuckles and bloodied fingernails. If you were to widen the poll to say eleven writers, you would get eleven different interpretations.

The beautiful thing about art is that each person brings their own self into the discussion—in this case, what is hope? Each author whose work appears in this anthology has taken their struggle with this question and revealed their heart through the veil of story. Then the reader picks up those stories and those answers become part of their experience. Engaging in the creative act, whether you are the creator or the receiver, allows us to enter into the never ending back-and-forth dance of co-creation. It's a practice that stretches across the barriers of time.

Even with this anthology, written and compiled in the year 2025, we continue the conversation with artists of the past. Not only in the authors who have shaped our own imagination who taught us how to craft a story, but specifically with two American artists; Emily Dickinson's words gave the anthology its name. Reading her entire poem invites us to grapple with the paradox of hope. In borrowing her words, we hearken back to her interpretation. The other artist we are in conversation with is Thomas Cole, who painted our chosen cover image The Voyage of Life: Manhood. The painting, which can be seen in the National Gallery of Art in Washington D.C., is one in a four part series depicting the pilgrimage of life. With its dark, moody browns and churning waters that contrast with the light of the seemingly aloof guide, Cole is also conveying that dichotomy of hope.

So we hope you not only enjoy these eleven stories, but that even one small aspect of their dance with hope shapes your own journey.

- *E.P. Fuselier, Co-founder of Inkwells & Anvils*

Story 1

The Waykeeper

S.J. Delacosta

The winds of time were ever-shifting—some days they whispered, others they spoke, yet others they roared. Humanity could do little but listen as they were caught up within them, a perpetual storm of first and last chances, hopes and dreams and endless possibilities begging to be grasped before scattering like dust. Elusive beasts moved within them, ferriers of fate and fortune rarely seen but ever-present. Their eyes were small as a man and large as an island, the flapping of their powerful wings enough to crush mountains.

In the eye of the storm, a lone waystation floated. Built upon the bones of a long-dead wind-beast—a desert island of dirt and stone sheltered from the tempest by the feathered turbine spinning below. It was a small place. A lonely place. But, in the isolation of the winds, a homely place. For those who sailed the winds, those who chose to break their currents and forge onwards into uncertain lands, it was a refuge, the last tethered stopping point in the known world.

It was the Waykeeper's duty to maintain the waystation and manage its operation. He was a haven master, a mechanic, a handyman, a rancher, an innkeeper, a weatherman, a signalman, and even a medic. However, at the moment, he felt like little more than a woefully afflicted maid.

A crew of windbreakers, blood hot with adventure, crowded the waystation's small inn, perched on tables and creaking windowsills, roaring and snoring in varying stages of inebriation. Their captain sat in a corner, deep in conversation with their guide, saying nothing to curb his crew's impertinence.

"Oi, Waykeeper!" a young windbreaker yelled, ale sloshing from his not-yet-empty tankard as he raised it. "More grog!"

The tankard slipped from clumsy fingers, scattering glass and ale across the floor the Waykeeper had only just that morning mopped. The final thread of his patience snapped.

"You've had more than enough to drink, ya damn hooligans!" He slammed his fists on the bartop. The guide, Myra, looked over with a raised brow at his display. He ignored her. "I'm closin' the bar!"

A concert of raucous hollers and whining moans accompanied his proclamation. With the single-minded disregard of a man who couldn't give less of a damn, he stepped out from behind the bar, cranking the mechanical wheel to drop the security screen and lock it shut.

"You can finish what you have and find your beds," he proclaimed, pocketing the key and striding towards the door.

"Cranky old coot," the windbreaker muttered. "What crawled up his ass and died?"

"Bet you'd be a cranky old coot, too, if you were stuck on this rock," another responded.

"What, it's not like no one's forcin' him to stay here. If he's so damn miserable, why doesn't he just up and leave?"

Yes, why don't *you?* the Waykeeper's mind mocked in his father's voice. He slammed the door behind him, Myra's knowing gaze burning a hole in his back.

Outside, it was blessedly quiet. Less than a mile from horizon to horizon, a wall of white surrounded him, a column of relative peace and tranquility. Only the whistling hum of the ever-spinning turbine was audible above the low, vibrating drone of the waystation's directional signal horns.

Waykeeper, Waykeeper, Waykeeper, Waykeeper, his mind chanted as he walked the winding path up towards the signal tower. He'd heard it so many damn times he'd nigh forgotten his own name.

Is that all you are now? Just a cranky old coot of a 'keeper with no aspirations of his own?

Memories flooded his mind, unprompted. His daughters, young and carefree; his wife joyous and beautiful; his home, filled with light and laughter and *clarity.* Back when he'd been someone, before he'd lost it all.

Before you threw it away.

He grit his teeth and paused his stride, balling his fists and turning his eyes heavenwards. How many nights had he spent alone, stuck, cursing the blood with which he'd been born for tethering him to this place? The Waykeeper's vision strayed towards the future, the years falling away until he was in his last. He saw himself crouching upon the cemetery ridge awaiting death—a lone, hunched shadow with only the silent bones of the dead for company.

He recoiled from the image, black terror gripping his soul, combing shaking fingers through his hair.

You need to get right with yourself. Find a purpose before life passes you by.

Above him, the night sky was spotted with stars, and the hulking forms of wind-beasts passed by, shadowing the white column of wind. He had never seen the full body of one, only illustrations brought back by windbreakers describing their encounters as nothing short of divine. Perhaps, if he could just catch a glimpse...

Shaking his head of fanciful notions, he continued onward.

* * *

"Boy! Get down here!"

Taking the steps two at a time, the young man flew through the door after his father as the bowsprit of a ship burst through the column of wind.

Why didn't they signal ahead?

Father and son barely reached the haven in time to deploy the emergency cradle before the badly damaged ship crashed into the dock. The wings across the flanks retracted, and the gangway was lowered, crew members spilling out.

"We were attacked by pirates," a harried windbreaker informed. "Captain's down and so's the first mate. We need immediate medical attention."

Two windbreakers rushed down the gangway carrying a stretcher. A young woman was laid upon it, flaxen hair clinging to her fever-slick brow, the crude bandages wrapped about her leg soaked through with blood.

"Grab me my medkit," his father ordered.

The young man ran to the dock house, fetching the medkit from the closet. He returned to find the woman sitting upright, arguing with her crewmates as they attempted to push her down. Two sky blue eyes, hazy with pain yet shining like topaz, raised to meet his own.

Oh, he realized, *she's beautiful.*

"No need to fret," he said, voice scratchy. Clearing his throat, he handed his father the medkit, dropping to one knee. "Old man knows his stuff. He'll have you back on your feet in no time."

The young woman giggled, a tinkling, musical sound.

"I'm Laiza," she said. "What's your name?"

He swallowed and took a breath, opening his lips to speak.

* * *

The Waykeeper made his way back down from the signal tower, his anger abated. Light still flickered in the inn's oil lamps, however the bar itself was empty. Myra's frame shadowed the doorway as she leaned against the jamb, arms crossed.

"They'll be heading out at first light," she said as he stepped into the lamplight. "Readings show they should have a good heading come morning."

"Faster they get outta my hair, sooner I'll get some peace and quiet," the Waykeeper groused.

Myra sighed. "They're a rowdy crew, but they're not scumbags. Captain had them mop up and offered to pay for damages. He wanted to stay up and apologize himself, but I told him I'd do it for him—he needs his sleep to be in top form tomorrow."

The Waykeeper considered her words. The Captain was young, but not inexperienced. Most of his crew, however, were untested. He wondered how well they'd fare once separated from their guide, if he'd ever see them again, or if they'd become yet another tale of cocksure windbreakers lost to the winds.

"I have some tea that should help with the hangovers," he said after a moment, "but stock's low. They'll have to ration it."

Myra raised a brow in surprise, before her lips curved into an approving smile. "I'm sure they'll appreciate that."

The Waykeeper grunted and headed down the path to his own empty bed.

* * *

"What do you do around here?" Laiza asked, hobbling ahead on her crutches, dodging rocks and crags with enviable ease.

"Nothing much, really." The young man shrugged his shoulders. "Maintain the grounds, maintenance the turbines, man the signal tower, manage the inn, keep the menagerie alive, that sort of thing."

"That sounds like a lot of work."

"I guess. Keeps us busy, at least."

Laiza hummed in response.

"You aren't upset they left you?" His voice dripped with skepticism. "They're probably off having some grand adventure. And you're...here." He gestured to the small, desert island around them. "Stuck."

"Sometimes adventure's a bit overrated." Laiza's smile was strained, eyes speaking of hidden pain. "Besides, it isn't too bad here, y'know."

"Really?" He scoffed incredulously.

She smiled at him, real this time, and so very beautiful. "You're here, after all."

Oh.

His heart skipped a beat.

* * *

The morning skies were clear, kissed by the first light of dawn, as the windbreakers prepared their ship. The Waykeeper finished his final checks, giving the crew the go-ahead. Myra stepped off the gangway, turning to the Captain, her salt-and-pepper braid whipping in the wind.

"This is where we part ways," she said.

"Thank you again for all your help," said the Captain. "We won't forget what you taught us."

"See that you don't. Your lives depend on it."

"I understand." He nodded gravely before lifting the gangway and sealing the hatch.

Air-ships were masterful works of engineering marvel with their carved wooden hulls lacquered with weather-resistant sealant, conical beaks forged from sleek brass jutting out from the bows and tapering to horizontal spires, dozens of decks and the men scurrying about them visible through the crystalline windows capping their portholes.

Large bone wings covered in the fledgling feathers of wind-beasts sprouting from the ship's flanks rose with a creaking *whoosh* as the windbreakers pulled ropes and turned wheels with choreographed efficiency. Wind buffeted the dock, and the low drone of the ship's brass horn reverberated through the air, the sheer force of it sending the dock to rattling and the Waykeeper's bones along with it. The ship burst forth by the pressure of sound, away from the waystation and towards the edge of the tempest. The wings caught a current, and the ship shot upwards and out, plunging bow-first into the winds, the crew cutting the wings to rigid airfoils. In less than a second, the ship was ferried from sight, the only evidence of its passing the low, brass note reverberating in its wake.

"Gorgeous, isn't it?" Myra watched on with soft sorrow. "This is her maiden voyage."

Might be her last, he thought grimly.

The crew were young. Reckless. Hot-blooded treasure hunters with more audacity than sense. He could only hope their aid had been sufficient to afford them a fighting chance.

"Well," said Myra, after a silent pause, "now that's handled, unlock your pantry, Waykeep! I've had enough breaker's stew to last me well into the grave."

He snorted, amused. For all her gray hairs and wrinkles, she really hadn't changed a bit. "I'll see what I can scrounge up."

The two fell into familiar step, and, for a moment, he could almost pretend the last decade had been nothing but a terrible dream.

* * *

"Good morning, good sir! What would you like for breakfast today?"

"Well, aren't you a charming lass." The supply ship captain's eyes twinkled with mirth. "What've you got for me?"

"Well," said the small girl with strawberry-blonde pigtails, "we have rhubarb pie, asparagus, eggs, and toast!"

"How about some eggs and asparagus for now and some pie for dessert."

"Of course!" The girl scribbled on her slate tablet, tongue sticking out in concentration. "Will that be all?"

"I think that's about good for now."

"Excellent! I shall pass your order on to the kitchen!"

"Much appreciated."

The Waykeeper watched his youngest daughter skip back into the kitchen where his eldest two were cooking up a storm.

"They're good girls," said Laiza with a smile.

They observed with amusement as their middle three moved about the room, taking orders, filling glasses, and ferrying plates to the twelve-man crew of the supply ship occupying the inn. They'd insisted on doing the breakfast call entirely themselves, and Laiza had talked him into letting them.

"A *handful,* is what they are," he grumbled fondly.

"You wouldn't have it any other way," his wife teased.

"Waykeep!" a supplyman called, raising his tankard. "More grog!"

His proclamation was met with cheers from the crew, and the girls giggled.

"Coming right up!" He smiled, Laiza a warm weight at his side.

Somehow, when he hadn't been looking, the lonely barren rock on which he'd been born and raised had become a home, and his father's bitter voice no longer echoed in the recesses of his mind.

"You know, I didn't expect to see you again," the Waykeeper admitted as he set to peeling potatoes. "I thought you'd retired."

"So did I." The guide's fingers were a flurry as she chopped radishes. "When Adam passed, Isaac and Cecelia still needed me, and it's hard to be a single mum from the decks of a ship. But they're grown now, and the winds call too loudly to ignore for long."

The Waykeeper frowned, talk of Myra's family drawing painful attention to the quiet emptiness of the waystation.

"Have you heard from them?" he asked. She'd known him long enough, he needn't specify who.

"Yes," she replied.

His hands paused. "How are they?"

"Well."

The room fell into silence punctuated by steady chopping.

His frown deepened. "Is that all you'll tell me?"

"They're good girls." *Chop.* "They don't deserve what you did to them."

"I know."

"*Do* you?" *Chop.* "You hurt them terribly. Marietta especially."

He pursed his lips, ashamed, but did not reply. The guide scoffed.

"I know I was a shit father," he said, after a moment of silence. "I couldn't give them what they wanted in this place."

"*No.*" She placed her knife on the cutting board, fixing him with a glare. "You were a *good* dad. Then you chose to be a prick. If you can't be bothered to write them all these years, you don't have a right to hear more."

"They're *my* daughters," he growled, slamming his fist against the wall. "I have *every* right!"

"You have a funny way of showing it." She sneered. "Now quiet down and peel your spuds or get out."

"This is *my* kitchen!"

"*Now.*"

The door rattled on its hinges as he slammed it shut with a resounding bang. He seethed as he marched up the stairs to his study, slamming books and scattering papers, until he'd calmed enough to turn his focus on the ledger that still needed updating. Uncapping his inkwell, he dipped his pen, and began to write.

Nearly an hour into his work, he heard footsteps approach.

"What?" he groused at the guide shadowing the doorsill of his study. "Is dinner ready?"

"Not yet," she said.

"Then why are you here?"

"Take a walk with me."

"After what you said?"

"A *walk,*" she reiterated, voice hard before sighing, the fight draining from her shoulders. "It's time we paid someone a visit."

* * *

It started with a tremor.

The Waykeeper was wiping tables, preparing for the evening meal rush, when he heard a sharp cry from the kitchen. Dropping his rag, he rushed in to see Marietta clutching her mother's bleeding hand.

"What happened?" he demanded, heart in his throat as he took Laiza's hand in his own.

"It's nothing," Laiza insisted, attempting to pull away. He did not let her. "The knife just slipped."

"Your hands were shaking," Marietta argued. "They've *been* shaking all evening."

"I'll be fine," Laiza insisted. "It's likely just exhaustion. We've had a busy week."

The Waykeeper wanted to argue, but he recognized the stubborn set of his wife's jaw and knew she would not listen.

"As soon as this is wrapped, you're going to rest. I'll call Elizabeth to help Marietta finish."

She relented reluctantly. However, even after her much-needed nap, the tremor persisted. A week later, she was bedridden with fever, and a week after that, her handkerchief was spotted with blood.

"I'm writing the doctor," he declared. Laiza was too weak to give more than a token protest.

"She's dying, isn't she," Marietta said as they watched the supply ship leave with a letter aboard. Even in the face of her mother's potential passing, her voice hardly wavered. However, he could tell from the tense line of her shoulders and the flatness of her expression that she was afraid.

"Not if I have anything to say about it," he'd responded.

It took the doctor two more months to make it, and by then it was far too late.

"She has a week left, maybe two," said Dr. Markus, grief weighing down his brow. He'd delivered all six of their daughters, been there for every round of shots and broken bones and wild pox. "The best I can do now is make her comfortable. I am sorry I can't do more."

"You did your best," he should have said, but the words would not come as color began to leech from his world.

A firm hand landed on his shoulder, squeezing. He found no comfort in its weight.

"Would you like to tell your daughters or shall I?"

"Do what you want," he said, brushing away the hand and stepping back into Laiza's room. "I'll be right here."

He had eyes only for his slumbering wife as the doctor left with a sigh.

* * *

The gravestone was getting old. He hadn't been by to visit since the day of her burial, and already the sun and rain had weathered it, softening the edges of the chiseled letters. A bouquet of flowers left in an upright vase—verbenas, her favorite—were withered and brown, long dead. He wrestled with the sight, memories of her still, cold body danced before his eyes. Taunting.

Myra placed a small bouquet of wildflowers upon the stone, touching her fingers to the engraved letters, before stepping back to stand beside him.

"Why do you stay?" she asked. "Your dad's dead. Wife dead. Drove your daughters away, even Marietta. No assistant to help out. Do you enjoy torturing yourself?"

"If you're going to scold me over my wife's grave, at least tell me something I don't already know," he shot back, but the fight had left him. He'd been avoiding this place, avoiding *her*. Laiza had always believed the best of him, but now…

"You really are a miserable old coot," Myra scoffed. "She'd be ashamed if she could see you now."

The words cut him to the quick. He sucked in a breath, sliding shaking hands into the pockets of his trenchcoat. "Why do you still guide?"

"It's in my blood," said Myra. "Been the family business for generations, and I don't feel quite right when I'm grounded."

The Waykeeper considered her answer before shaking his head, scowling. "I hate it here."

"Then why stay?"

"Where else would I go?" He raised his arms. "This is the only life I've ever known. And my daughters clearly hate me now."

"They don't hate you," she said quietly. "They're hurt and they're angry, but they don't hate you."

"Then why won't you tell me more?"

"Why won't you apologize?"

"Would they even accept an apology from me?"

She was quiet for a moment, gaze distant.

"I can't tell you for certain…but I know they still love you. It may take time, but you need to be the one to move first."

His hands balled into fists, feet firmly rooted.

Stuck. *Always* stuck.

"What—" He swallowed thickly. "What if I can't?"

"Then you'll die here alone," her words rang with finality, "like you've always feared."

His vision strayed in time, and a lone shadow materialized upon the ridge. He raised his gaze to meet it, black terror reflecting the deepest corners of his soul. It was chilling. Petrifying. He desperately wished to turn his head, hide from the grim omen. The inevitable future.

Move.

He didn't look away.

The shadow wavered.

* * *

Death came for everyone. It was a fact with which he was intimately familiar as a keeper of the last waystation in the known world. However, Laiza had been life incarnate, a bright star that shone with such brilliance, he didn't believe it could ever be extinguished. He didn't know how to live without her. He'd never imagined he'd have to learn how.

"Dinner's ready." His eldest daughter's voice, muffled through the door. "Would you please come out?"

He should answer. It was what a good father would do. However, it was as though his voice had left him alongside his wife. His lips remained still.

"Elizabeth made roasted duck," Marietta continued. "Katya even garnished the salad just like Mama used to."

The memory stabbed him like a knife, but the pain was muted as his mind drifted far above the waystation.

"*Please*," she begged. "We need you, Dad. *I* need you. I...I'm trying my best, but I can't do it all on my own. *Please* come out."

He blinked, eyes slipping towards the window, towards the wall of white. The girl's sobs were quiet things, her retreating footsteps like the pitter patter of raindrops as the heavens opened, drowning the world in drab gray.

* * *

Alone at last, he mused with bitter irony as he watched the supply ship leave, the guide's parting words ringing in his ears.

"*Write them,*" she'd said before stepping onto the gangway. "*You owe them that, at the very least.*"

Once the ship disappeared from sight, he meandered about the grounds, throwing himself into his chores. The sun was low by the time he finished, and he hesitated exiting the menagerie gate, uncertain.

You're stalling.

Gathering his courage, he headed to his study. Clearing away the mess of ledgers and logs scattered about, the Waykeeper sat down, pulling a sheaf of paper from his drawer. He placed a page on his desk, uncapping his inkwell to dip the nib of his pen. The face of his youngest swam through his mind as he wrote her name in looping script.

Dear Annabelle,

I hope this letter finds you well. It has been many years since I last saw your face and I think of you every day...

He wrote long into the night. First Annabelle then Katya then Noella then Natalia then Elizabeth. He poured his heart and soul upon the pages, recounting stories of their childhood joys and misadventures, painting pictures with his words. He asked after their lives, and then told them of his—of windbreakers that had passed through, of the exotic creatures they'd added to the menagerie, of the time he'd shared with his old friend before she'd departed.

Five completed letters, enveloped and sealed with wax, lined the edge of his desk.

He lifted the next page from the stack and paused, freshly-dipped pen hovering. The blank page glared at him accusingly as he tried to form words that refused to come. The others had arisen so easily, gushing forth from his nib as they never had from his lips.

He pressed the nib to the page and began to write.

Dear Marietta,

How are you?

He frowned. No, that wasn't quite right. Too demanding. He crossed it out.

I've been thinking of you.

No, too insipid. Marietta had always hated platitudes.

I haven't heard from you in a while.

No, that was wrong. Sounded far too much like one of his own father's guilt trips.

He scowled, crumpling the page and tossing it across the room. It hit the wall and fell to the floor with a soft plop. Dozens more joined it before the waystation was again illuminated by the rays of first light.

The sixth envelope remained unfilled.

Noella was the first to leave, gone one night without a word leaving bitter silence and broken hearts in her wake. Natalia was close behind, unable to bear living in a home without her twin. Katya left next, taking Annabelle with her, tears streaming down his youngest's face as they'd boarded the ship bound for the mainland. That was the night he'd finally broken his cardinal rule, the burn of liquor chasing away the sight of his daughter's tears as he drank until he could remember no more.

Elizabeth lasted another year, but the Waykeeper knew she'd only stayed for Marietta who continued to man the waystation by his side, even as her sisters departed. However, not even Marietta could keep Elizabeth tethered forever, and when she left, it was in the arms of a strapping young windbreaker who'd made his fortune on the winds.

The quiet itched at the Waykeeper's nerves, picked and scratched and tore until they were open and raw and volatile. He had sworn he would never become the bitter, hateful man his father had, yet his fingers invariably found their way around the neck of a bottle night after night as Marietta alone kept the waystation from falling to ruins.

"I hate it here," he spat, already two bottles deep.

"This is the first I hear of it," Marietta snarked.

"Don't get smart with me, girl. This place is a prison."

"So you always tell me." She extinguished the last of the oil lanterns.

"The only thing that made it bearable was Laiza," he griped. "Now that she's dead, there's nothing here for me."

Silence, for a moment, punctuated only by the sound of their breaths.

"I suppose there's not," she said, barely above a whisper.

When the next supply ship pulled out of the haven with his daughter aboard, he was well and truly alone.

* * *

The winds of time were ever-shifting—some days they whispered, others they spoke, yet others they roared. But they had never sounded quite like *this*.

Desert shrubs bowed and snapped in the wind. The waystation flag was ripped from its pole, and bolted shutters rattled in their frames. The low drone of the signal tower rose with eerie intensity as the rushing winds scattered the sound this way and that. The turbine roared as it spun faster and faster to oppose the unprecedented gale.

What god had humanity angered to visit such wrath upon them? Was this chastisement for their hubris in choosing to break the winds? Or was this his own personal penance for the pain he'd caused his family?

The Waykeeper crouched low to the ground as he hurried towards the engine house. He crashed through the door, bolting it shut and lighting the gas lamp at the top of the spiral staircase. His feet moved with swift surety as he rushed down the familiar iron steps, the sound of the winds growing fainter, but the roar of the turbine amplifying until he could hear nothing over it. It pressed upon his ears, pounding a punishing rhythm against the bone of his skull as he stepped off onto a broad catwalk.

Below him, a vortex of feathers whirled, and he clutched the railing with both hands, muscles straining to keep his knees from buckling. A snap, loud as lightning, ripped through brass as the catwalk tore in half like a sheet of paper. He scrambled for purchase as the debris was sucked down into the raging vortex. The turbine stuttered, screeching and grinding as it slowed. It halted, gears straining, debris wedged between the hub and blades.

In the sudden silence, he heard it, the call of a ship's horn signaling its approach. His eyes widened in horrified realization just as the winds hit, and his world became blindingly white.

Yefrem...

He floated in a blank space, weightless, eyes both open and closed, body wrapped in a cushion of fuzz, swaddling him like a babe...

Yefrem...

A sound, deep and low, echoing and musical. It came from everywhere and nowhere at once, filling his head before his ears and carving through his skin to nestle deep within his bones...

Yefrem...

Yefrem. That was his name. It had been so long since anyone had spoken it, he'd nearly forgotten...

Yefrem!

An eye, large as a mountain was tall, blinked open, emerging from the sea of white. It was a glittering prism of color that pierced his very soul, flaying him in an instant until he was laid bare, unable to hide even the darkest parts of himself. Around the eye, the whiteness rippled—feathers, sleek and bright and perfectly aligned.

What are you? he asked, though his lips did not move.

I am the one who governs the winds: the ferrier of fate and fortune, the guide of the traveler, the refuge of the lost, the scourge of the wicked. I am the Way, and I chose you to be my Keeper.

His soul trembled.

Why me? he pleaded. *I am nothing—a failure of a man. Why not another?*

I do not wish to choose another. I want you. The words were like lightning, rumbling and electric, coursing through him. *Will you trust me?*

Trust...

Trust was harsh hands and cutting words, cold stone and heavy hearts, rancid breath and broken promises. Trust had left him a damaged shell, bitter and alone.

And yet...

Trust was soft smiles and tinkling laughter, youthful antics and a crowded home, meals shared and letters written. Trust was pain, yes, but it was also its remedy.

I don't know if I can...but I'll try.

Then go. Keep the way.

The eye blinked shut.

Sound rushed back to his ears with a sudden pop, and he was once again aware of his body, hands gripping the railing as the storm winds raged below him out of control. He was back where he had been, however he was not alone. That presence remained at the edge of his conscience, nudging him forward.

Trust me, Yefrem.

Letting go of the railing, he rushed down the catwalk, towards the torn edge. He spun a dial and tossed a lever before grabbing the winch chain and leapt. Air rushed past him as he dove. He could barely see through the raging winds, but he felt the presence teaching him to read the currents, the path through becoming brilliantly clear.

His feet landed on the hub with a crash, and he fought for purchase as he secured the chain about the debris. He waited with bated breath as the mechanical system reacalibrated, and the chain snapped taut. With a screeching of metal that set his teeth on edge, the debris was ripped upwards and outwards, nearly taking his head with it.

The turbine roared to life.

Yefrem clutched the rungs of the access ladder as the turbine spun, waging a war against the howling winds, until at last they were back under its control. The air cleared, and he could see it again—the wall of white ringing the waystation. Over the rushing of wind and the roaring of the turbine, came the call of a ship's horn. A brass spire emerged, the wooden hull of a ship breaking through the winds, wings unfurling.

Relief chased away his adrenaline. *They're safe.*

Yefrem felt a nudge, deep within his soul. Fixing his gaze upon the hulking form shadowing the column of wind, he was overcome with gratitude. "Thank you."

The wind caressed his hair, tender as a mother's touch. Yefrem basked in the sensation for a moment, then turned his attention upwards. He had a ship to dock, a meal to cook, a crew to attend, and a letter to write.

Grasping the rungs of the ladder tight, he climbed.

Story 2

Watercolors

Caspar

She would forgive him. She always had.

So thought Daniel as he hurriedly locked his apartment door and stepped out into the grey of morning in the city. It was overcast, but not ominously so; he thought about turning around for his beloved Totoro umbrella, but decided against it. It was only a twenty-minute walk to Hannah's apartment after all, and given the way things had ended last night she might not find the gesture of using the gift as romantic as she normally insisted she did.

Daniel was the sort of man who liked to walk. Difficult not to be, in a borough like Dismas Ridge, where ancient knots of streets and historical-society-preserved creaking tetracentennial buildings made the idea of train or bus lines a bad joke; it made even car transit sometimes the slowest route between two points. Hannah had called the Ridge 'the past's revenge on the ambitions of the future,' once. Daniel didn't share her grievances; but then, he hadn't needed to give up an oversized SUV to move here. For him, the crooked garrets, the eclectic turnings of the byways, the gargoyles nested among satellite dishes—these were all home, as natural as the city mists or the croaking of the ravens.

He set out at a brisk pace, tracing the route in his head. Two rights, a left, straight through the park, then it was there on the right. Daniel had always had a good head for space. That, plus a penchant for going to college with the right people, had brought him into the design world that he had cheerfully inhabited for over a decade now. He could envision the route clearly, pulsing blue on the map of the Ridge that Daniel kept tucked away in a drawer in his mind.

The street was empty—not unusual, given the early hour and the ugly weather. Daniel's neighborhood was on the better end of the economic scale, peopled largely by folks working in the sort of job that doesn't require you to be up terribly early. Hannah hated that, he reflected ruefully, but it was hardly his fault that he was doing well for himself. She acted as though prosperity were a crime.

A fat drop of rain splashed against his cheek. Another. So, the ambivalent clouds had made up their mind. At least there would be no nervous anticipation. Daniel didn't mind getting wet; he hadn't brought his phone in his rush for the door, and the mild discomfort might help clarify his rushing thoughts. As the sky committed, accelerating from a spatter to a drizzle to a firm but light rain, Daniel tried to hammer out precisely what he would say when he arrived.

Waking up to that sort of voicemail was impossible. *Leaving town for good, don't talk to me again, early flight. I hate you. It was never real.* The human heart wasn't built to take in that sort of poison, let alone before someone had even brushed their teeth, before the fog of sleep had lifted from the brain's streets.

He didn't think that he'd done anything worthy of the condemnation he'd received. So he'd said a few offhand comments after one too many vodka seltzers. Hannah could hardly hold that against him, let alone so violently abandon the fragile thing they had been building together.

"And why should I apologize, anyhow?" Daniel groused quietly.

When he arrived at her apartment, he wouldn't apologize after all —in fact, he would demand an apology himself before insisting on helping her carry her bags to the airport. Chivalry wasn't dead and all that. He couldn't allow himself to be a doormat, to put up with that torrent of abuse for what was, after all, a few harmless lines, when she had *known* he was rather merry.

The rain picked up. It was coming down hard now, slamming into the paving stones, the audible drumming sending up little ricochets of spray. What little foot traffic there had been scattered for the sundry cafes and upscale restaurants that lined Park Street. Daniel cursed himself for not having the good sense to be among their number, as the wet began to soak through the seams of his battered overcoat. Perhaps he could...but no. This needed to be addressed, for the sake of closure. If he saw a cab, he could hail one, but other than that, he was locked into the walk.

He made the first right turn. Visibility was declining, as the wet grey curtain of heavy rain closed in on all sides. He could hardly see the buildings across the road, could scarcely make out the men and women huddled around their laptops and lattes through the plate glass of the coffee shops.

Ah, well. It would be good for the plants.

That's what Hannah would say about it, anyhow. Hannah, with her odd habits and love of greenery, who so struggled with the City's stone. They had met on one of his walks, a 3 a.m. encounter in the heart of Ridgeline Park. Both terrified of the other at first, both out alone in the mist, the only way to process the sort of heavy feelings that can't quite be processed indoors. He, mulling on a bad breakup; she, uncertain if she had made the right choice in moving here to begin with. Once they had realized that each had no intention of stabbing the other, they'd had a remarkable near-instant bond, talking for hours sitting on the swings in the park. It's remarkable how effective the mirror a stranger holds up can be in processing your own feelings.

She had come here for a landscaping project—or, as she called it, "beautification," something about building parks in the less upscale districts of the city, off of the Ridge, where sunlight was a scarcer commodity and where few had the luxury of escaping the omnipresent rain. Hannah had a habit of narrating her origin story the same way every time—always remarking how the images she had seen of tenements and shattered windows had ripped her heart out. She was brought in from outside, accepted against her better judgment. It was slow, ugly, bureaucratic work, getting the thing going.

A distant flash, a distant crash. The rain was coming down in sheets, waves, crashing against the pavement. This couldn't be safe, he mused distantly. But he could get out of the rain at Hannah's. Surely she wouldn't deny him that basic dignity. Visibility was even worse, somehow. The opposite side of the street was invisible now, concealed behind the rain curtain and a dense fog or mist that permeated everything.

"Was that possible?" he wondered. "Could it truly be so opaquely foggy and raining so intensely simultaneously?" Yet so it was. No sense in arguing with physical reality.

His foot splashed into a deceptively deep puddle off the curb, soaking his jeans nearly to the knee. He cursed. Still, the shock was focusing, as he had hoped. He had hoped for this effect, but that felt like a stranger's decision, a distant report from far-away lands.

The crux, then. The thing he would need to justify in his closing remarks to Hannah. Yesterday had been bad, for other reasons that he couldn't quite recall at this moment. He had come into the dinner angry. The drinks—he couldn't recall how many. Too many. What had he said exactly?

"Stop complaining about your pointless work."

Another crash of thunder.

In his office, with the company he worked for—surely he should remember that name—they had a tradition, around Christmas, of a gift exchange. A so-called White Elephant, a gift swap. Out of curiosity, he had looked into the origin of the name. Once upon a time, somewhere less fortunate, the king would give subjects that he did not like white elephants as gifts. This was a faux-gift, a trap. For reasons of religion, the elephant could not be slaughtered or given away, and was ruinously expensive to care for. The White Elephant was a gift that killed.

Self-knowledge is such a gift.

He sensed, on an animal level, the choices before him, forking like the prongs of lightning lancing through the grey of the city sky. He looked around furtively, seeking a geographical escape from the purely mental trap. The animal instinct to recoil from the awareness of his wrongdoing, to find excuses for his behavior. After all, he *had* been at less than his best, and surely Hannah must know that her work couldn't ever really make a difference.

And yet. There was some other, deeper instinct to tear open the rent in his self-image, to explore the full extent of the rot that had taken root. He made a feeble attempt to shove his rain-drenched locks out of his face, only for them to slide back into place. He smiled ruefully.

"Well, what else is a walk in the rain for but navel gazing?" he muttered. He couldn't hear himself over the water pounding off the cobbles.

He took the next right.

The curtain of rain blocking his vision was only feet away now. He traveled in a bubble of visibility, a dot of color in an ocean of grey, where the sky and the ground and the walls were nigh-indistinguishable. He glanced to his right, only for mild curiosity and major discomfort to fade away into something else entire.

There was something viscerally...wrong with the laptopers and coffee-drinkers, something wavery and indistinct, even through the curtain. They seemed made of smoke, or of paint dissolving in water. Insubstantial. Absent, almost. He stopped in front of the next place he passed.

The sign was smeared, unreadable, advertising what looked to be "CWFEY" and "HF OOP." The door would not open. He knocked. Nobody looked up from their screens, their conversation partners, their coffee. He tugged again. The knob felt slightly rubbery in his wet hand, the brass squishing inwards more than it should. Nothing.

He knocked on the plate glass. No response. A damp, pathetic "Hello?" Useless. The smokey, vague patrons continued to stare at screens that seemed covered in nonsense, garbled walls of lorem ipsum done in impressionist watercolors.

He backed away slowly and turned back to his route, trying to tamp down his rising panic. He tried self-deception on for size. Surely they just couldn't hear him in the storm. The howling and pounding of the winds were loud enough to obliterate any noise he could make. He hadn't yelled, hadn't wanted to look crazy around people he might know. What sort of madman screamed just because of a bit of rain? Perhaps he had taken ill from the drenching he was suffering through, and some sort of fevered hallucination was at work.

Yet, in truth, it was none of these paltry excuses that distracted the man from his concerning physical surroundings. Rather, it was the yawning portal that had opened up inside him, the terrible gulf that reexamination of memory was ripping through his sense of self.

He considered his opinion of Hannah through the months they had been together. Had he always been so contemptuous of her work? He had, the man realized. It wasn't anything personal or specific to her or her specific type of do-gooding. It was simply the sort of condescending smirk that one must give to the sort of person Hannah was. Naive, idealistic, salvatory, as if the work of any one person could really move the needle. Not to mention the more subtle, bitter notes of resentment; people like her always seemed to think they were better than people like him, didn't they? Why would they do that sort of work if not to exalt themselves, to set themselves on pedestals far above the mere mortals that made up the rest of the species? No, he had decided, her work was clearly a waste of time, an ego-trip distraction from the real work that the rest of the species needed to get on with.

He had always felt this way about Hannah's dreams of building, of renewing. Egotistic and pointless. He had just kept those thoughts locked inside, until a bad day at work and ten vodka seltzers had unlocked a door that he had thought more securely sealed.

But now, locked in the storm and in his wet body, he forced himself to reckon with the follow-on. "Was I the jerk, after all?" he mused quietly, no longer concerned about the judgment of the smoke-stains in the false smudges of the nameless buildings he passed. His voice was muddy, a creek choked with debris, syllables slurring into one another and out of comprehension. "Maybe I wasn't fair. Maybe."

He took the left into the park. Crossing the street was like fording a river, nearly a foot of water flooded the avenue. Obviously, manifestly unsafe. Yet he kept wading, though he could not see the road or the cars or the sky or the pavement or...anything. Twenty, thirty, forty feet in a world made only of steel-grey and misery. The street wasn't this wide, was it? It was impossible to tell, impossible to locate himself without a referent, impossible to tell if he was actually making any progress through the cold and the wet.

And then he was through, all at once, boots slapping onto pavement, squelching into the mud of the park. He glanced up at the sign. The letters were smeared beyond recognition, "Ridgeline Park" rendered a ragged line of white on green. Worse, drops of white had fallen off the sign, spattering on the ground. He hadn't realized that the park's construction had been so shoddy; he would have made a note to write to someone and complain, had he not been so preoccupied.

For this park, where he had met Hannah, brought the man's mind more fully into focus. Focus on the woman he had known, the beauty of her laugh, the impishness of her sense of humor, her love of long walks, her taste in movies (good) and takeout (terrible). They had not dated for long, but they had dated deeply, and the man felt that he knew her well enough to say: she was sincere. Nothing about her spoke of hypocrisy, of egoism, of naiveté. She did not fit into the framework the man had pre-assigned her, but he had put her there anyway.

And if he was wrong about that...

He jumped back as a tree limb fell across his path, splattering wetly on the ground. It was liquifying rapidly, running into a stream of brown sludge under the force of the rain. The trees around him were sagging, slumping into themselves as the rain tore at their form. Something was very, very wrong.

He shouted for help. The sound was weak, tinny, useless. He was in the middle of a park in the middle of the worst storm he had ever seen. Who would come?

But it was worse than that. He realized with horror that his voice was garbled, inchoate. It still sounded like language, but less so than it should. He touched his throat. It *gave* slightly under his touch, squishing inwards in a way that healthy flesh simply did not.

He was near a lumpy structure, brown brick that used to be a... building, probably. An awning remained, sheltering a pool somehow sedate in the storm. He considered the prospect of even marginal shelter and took a half-step towards the puddle. And he saw what he was.

The ink-smudge people behind the panes of the false-lying shops, the screen-people pretending to occupy untrue space had become him. Or him them. Did it make a difference? He was blurred, skin and clothes and hair spiraling out like paint dissolving in water, tendrils of self forming new shades with the brick and ground and water. And his face—his *face*—nobody could bear—he could not—

"NO!" shouted through liquid lungs, sounding like whale song, mournful and meaningless.

He ran.

He ran through mud and liquid grass and melting stones, past puddles that once were trees, hearing no sound but the rain and the rain and the rain. He ran on legs that weakened, then softened, then gave out. And then, he crawled. He crawled for what felt like hours, but simultaneously he knew could not have been more than a few minutes. He dragged himself forwards until, unaccountably, he reached a solid object.

A swing. A child's swing, part of a set, unmelted, unsmeared, a vibrant, inviting yellow against the endless grey. He hauled his liquid body up into the seat and stopped. This would be the end, he real-ized. He could not possibly reach Hannah's apartment, not in his state of dissolution. He couldn't feel his legs, couldn't feel his torso—the man realized with a start that he couldn't remember his name.

Perhaps it was for the best. As far as the man knew, the only option after realizing yourself to be a monster was self-annihilation. Melting like this was seemingly painless. Cheaper than a case of vodka seltzers, anyhow.

"Tough night?"

A woman's voice, from the swing next to him. He had no neck anymore, and could not look to see who it was.

"You could say that. I feel like I'm falling apart." He realized with pleasant shock that he could be heard, though perhaps his body wasn't what was conveying sound anymore.

"It's funny you say that." The woman's voice, wry. "So am I. Something about this rain—it seems to, uh, dissolve you. Sorry, does that sound crazy? I feel a little crazy, saying it out loud. But honestly, I'm just glad to have a voice right now."

"No, no, I get it!" the man said. "I'm right there with you. I don't remember what—I just know that I screwed up. Screwed up bad. It's honestly a relief to be able to tell someone that, even if it's just trauma-dumping on a stranger."

"It's alright," the woman said, answering the unspoken query. "I'll take a turn after you. Besides, what's the harm? We'll both end up puddles anyhow." The mist somehow snuck a smile into the remark, hints of personality not erased.

"Emotionally fulfilled puddles, right? That's something...but yeah. Now this woman I've been seeing is leaving, leaving for good, and I feel like I'm thunder."

"Like you're thunder? What, like you're noisy? You scare dogs?" the woman's voice laughed.

The man laughed as well, bitterness mixed with joy. He didn't know how he could be talking right now, but delight at being able to make noise mingled with the hopelessness of the situation. "No, like

I'm showing up with a warning five seconds too late. The lightning already hit, and I'm shouting about how to make it right."

"No chance you can tell her you're sorry?"

"Not without legs. What about you? What took you out into the body-melt?"

"Opposite problem, I guess. I was lightning to my poor guy. I dumped this loser—rightfully so, I think. He was—he wasn't what I thought. But now, right at the edge of moving on, I keep thinking of all his other qualities. He wasn't just the worst parts of him, y'know? The guy didn't get my work—not that I can remember what it is right now—but he was kind, funny, sweet. The sort of man you just know, deep down, is better than the ideas he's absorbed from his idiot friends and lifestyle, if only you could drag him out of his shell. It's like, hey moron, I love you, let's go see the world together so you get some damn perspective and stop running your mouth about things. But instead, he broke my heart, and I said a lot of things intended to hurt him in return, and now I don't know what to do with myself. Does that make sense?"

Daniel felt solidity pulse through him, a wave of warmth and stability pushing out from his chest. He looked over—was able to look over—at the woman, saw only a brown mist floating in the other swing. They were all alone, on the candy-yellow swings, floating in a grey, wet void. The ground had disappeared long ago, soaked into nothingness by the dissolving damp.

"Yeah, it does, actually," he said. "You know—and I'm just a stranger in the park, so take this with a whole shaker of salt—but I'd be willing to bet that you might have been the lightning that idiot needed..." He shifted awkwardly on the swings, becoming pleasantly aware of the unpleasant sensation of a soaked but real body.

Daniel sighed and soldiered on: "...even if you said it in a harsh way. Honestly, especially because you did. Realizing that you're wrong is...I'm sorry, Hannah. You were right. You should leave me, but you deserve to know that." More wetness on his face, salty. Just as the rain seemed to finally be letting up.

Sound returned like a thief, details creeping in as the roar of wind and crash of water began their long ebb. Above, around, new shades cracked the dome of grey, blacks and blues and greens infiltrating the palette.

In the other swing, the mist began to solidify. The familiar outline coalesced: the ragged dirty-blond hair with the white streak she *swore* she'd dyed that way on purpose, the stocky, surprisingly muscular build, the familiar paint-stained jacket. As the rain drizzled to a gentle stop, Daniel saw Hannah clearly.

Story 3

That My Foes May See

Grace F. Hopkins

The door to the inn bangs open with the force of the wind and a shove from behind.

All is dark and quiet as the girl stumbles, panting, over the threshold, rain-soaked hair dripping water down her face. The innkeeper behind the counter startles at the sight of her and her traveling companion, both gasping and soaked to the bone.

She is too weary to form even a greeting, so it is her companion who steps forward first, his priest's cassock muddy at the hem, streaming water.

"Please," he says to the innkeeper behind the bar, his voice breathless. "Do you have rooms?" The words come slowly, trippingly, his tongue meant for another language.

The innkeeper looks as if he intends to say 'no,' but his eyes fall on the girl, as a shiver races down her spine. She clutches at the bulge at her midsection and sways involuntarily on her feet. Tears mingle with the rain on her face.

His eyes soften. Grudgingly, he shows them the stairs.

When she is alone, she strips off her sopping dress. It falls around her ankles, and out from underneath tumbles her spare dress, her prayer book wrapped inside, damp, but thankfully spared from the worst of the rain. Everything in her pack has long been soaked through.

She pulls on the spare dress, and has just finished combing through her tangled locks when there is a tentative knock.

She opens the door a crack and peeks around it, but it is only the priest on the other side. She opens it wider.

"May I come in?" Fr. Gerebran asks. "I was hoping you'd join me for night prayer."

She steps aside and then shuts the door behind them both.

His black cassock also smells musty, both with sea-water and rain. But it must have been his spare because he's not nearly as wet as he had been a half hour ago. He smells faintly of anointing oil.

"I hope you don't mind being a recent widow," he says as he crosses toward the little window and sits on a low stool by the wall. "I'm taking you to stay with relatives—or at least, that's the impression I gave." He winks at her.

She knows Father does what he can to avoid lying outright, but their travels have been nothing but a mess of half-truths meshed together with the assumptions of others. When they'd first left Oriel, Fr. Gerebran had worn the clothes of a farmer, and he'd treated her as his daughter. He'd since given away his lay clothes to a beggar they'd met on the road. Now it was his duty to concoct a reason why a priest was traveling alone with a young woman at each place they stopped. After all, her true father was likely to have noticed that Fr. Gerebran had disappeared the same night she did. He would be looking for them both.

"We can decide different aliases at the next town, if you like." He fishes in his pocket and produces a bread roll. He holds it out to her.

She strides forward and sits on the end of the lone, low-slung bed. She takes it. It's still warm to the touch.

"I was just downstairs," Fr. Gerebran says. "The innkeeper wanted me to anoint his mother; she's got a terrible fever. But his wife was very insistent that I bring this extra bread for *you*. I think our hosts are under the impression you're with child."

She balks at that, unsure whether to feel amused or guilty. She'd merely intended to keep her belongings dry, not pass herself off as a pregnant mother. But if her actions have given her a disguise and earned them a little extra kindness, she supposes she must be thankful for it.

She's played many roles since she left home.

For the first leg of their trip she had been the deaf daughter to Fr. Gerebran's farmer, pretending not to hear any of the fellow travelers they met on the road. Aboard the ship they'd taken to this continent, she'd been an eager postulant on her way to a foreign convent. But tonight, she supposes a pregnant widow will suffice.

After all, anything is better than the truth. And the further from the truth, the better. As long as no one here can identify her as the runaway princess of Oriel, as long as their pursuers can't follow the tracks of her various aliases—they are safe. For she knows it is not a matter of *if* her father would set to tracking her down, it is only a matter of *when*.

Consider this God's Providence, she tells herself, and takes a bite of the bread. She rips off half and holds it out toward Father.

But he doesn't notice, for he has pulled his prayer book from his pocket and is leafing through it, looking for the proper page. By the light of the room's lone candle, she realizes for the first time how *spent* he looks. It is as if she can see every groove of his face, every stray strand of grey that has begun to pepper his hair.

A gratitude for him wells, along with concern. He's given everything he has to keep her safe these past weeks, even at so high a cost. She needs him to keep his stamina up—they still have so far to go.

She nudges him with the back of her hand.

He looks up from his book. "Oh," he says. "No thank you."

She raises an eyebrow, and with an acquiescing smile, he takes her offering, blesses it, and eats. Once he's swallowed, he looks up at her, and, stifling a yawn, says, "Shall we begin?"

* * *

"In the day of distress I will call and surely you will reply," Fr. Gerebran recites, the pages of his prayer book rustling under his fingertips. *"Among the gods there is none like you, O Lord; nor work to compare with yours."*

They had read this psalm at her mother's funeral, naught but a year before. She can hardly recite it without thinking of that day now. It had been raining then, too. And Fr. Gerebran had been the one to intone the psalm at the graveside. She'd stood close to him, hoping his figure could eclipse her from the view of her father who waited outside the ring of mourners like some dark wraith, watching, but not joining in the funeral proceedings.

The timing of it had been cruel. A girl her age needed a mother. But especially she—a Christian in a castle full of pagans—needed her mother more than ever. Her mother's death meant that she'd lost her protector, her advocate, the only person who had ever been able to convince the king of anything.

"For your love to me has been great. You have saved me from the depths of the grave..."

On the night of her mother's funeral, she had woken to the sound of slaughter.

She'd watched from the window as her father and his collection of black-clad druids had crowded around the freshly turned earth of her mother's grave.

And they, in their crude masks and harsh chants and guttural cries, had emptied the blood of a goat onto the new headstone.

Her father could coat the whole castle in blood, and it wouldn't bring her mother back. But, if she knew anything about her father, it was that he intended to try.

It began to storm, and though the torches guttered, their dark ritual continued. Animals upon animals were lined up for execution. And the rain ran red with blood.

"The proud have risen against me; ruthless men seek my life; to you they pay no heed."

There was no storm greater than a king in mourning. In the weeks that followed, her father raged and skulked around the castle, his temper and moods as mercurial as spring skies. For her father is nothing if not relentless. Stubborn. And his wife was the first thing that'd ever been taken from him that he hadn't been able to reclaim.

It had destroyed him.

Sometimes on her way in or out of the castle, he would find her and seize her, like a hound upon a forest hare. He would either rage at her God, rough hands encircling her arms so tightly that bruises formed, or he'd hold her in such a desperate, sobbing crush that she was winded and perturbed by the intensity of his display.

Sometimes, when he held her to him, he murmured apologies, and oaths, and wishes into her hair that were meant for her mother alone—as if she, who bore her mother's eyes and dark tresses, were to also bear her place.

So she made herself scarce. She spent long days in the wood, or hiking the hill toward the priory where Fr. Gerebran or his brother priests received her and let her while away afternoons praying in their chapel or laboring in their garden in exchange for supper. Were she not a girl, she would have begged them to take her as a seminarian. Anything to escape the thunderheads of her father's grief.

For her one place of solace inside the castle—her little chapel—her father had already sealed off. Perhaps because it reminded him of his late wife. Perhaps because, while he tolerated her and her mother's Christianity while she was still alive, he had no need to tolerate it in her death.

So at night she knelt before her little icon of the Virgin and her gilt crucifix and begged them to banish the darkness from this house. For each day that passed she had an unnerving premonition that a yet more vicious tempest was brewing and soon it would swallow her whole.

"O give your strength to your servant and save your handmaid's son."

* * *

It had been another stormy night not quite a month ago when Fr. Gerebran knocked on the door to her bedchamber with none of the softness and hesitancy he did tonight.

She'd been surprised to see him standing at the threshold, rain-soaked and frantic. He'd never visited her here before—he hardly came to the castle now that the chapel was bricked shut, least of all to her own bed-chamber. But something in the look on his face compelled her to let him in with no questions, and as quietly as possible.

Once the door was closed, he leaned against it and met her with a gaze so stern and striking that she forgot about the strangeness of the visit and instead fought down a panic rising in her throat.

"I'm so sorry," he said, eyes glistening, voice shaking. "But my dear princess, I have come to tell you that you are in great danger."

She had known this already, had felt it in her bones ever since that night she'd seen her father and his druids enact the devil's sacrament. To hear Fr. Gerebran confirm it now was almost a relief. Her anticipation was finally manifesting into *something*.

"What do you know?" she whispered.

Fr. Gerebran closed his eyes and forced the words past his lips as if loathing that he had to be the one to speak such damning news. "It's your father. He means to take you for a wife."

She stumbled backwards into her bedframe, and gripped a post for support. Her stomach churned with revulsion. "No. It can't be. Why...why *me*?"

Fr. Gerebran's brow was furrowed and his jaw set. When he spoke, his words dripped with repressed anger. "I cannot fathom the full workings of his mind. He means to marry again—he still lacks a male heir. But even now he longs for your mother. He sees her when he looks at you, and I do not think that he is sane enough anymore to tell the difference."

It felt so raw and horrible to hear her worst fears come from his mouth. She had suspected such things on a deep and intuitive level—all the times he'd cornered her and grabbed her with a touch too brazen, a passion too strong. But she had sequestered such a cruel and horrible notion to the very back of her mind lest even thinking of it bring it to fruition.

"But I'm his *daughter*."

"I know."

"And I'm a virgin." Her words were a plea, a strangled prayer whispered between them.

Not only had she never known man, she never intended to, either. She nervously twisted the slim ring on her left hand. It was more than a trinket. It was a vow. A symbol of that which she had given to her beloved Jesus that she intended to give to no earthly husband. When her mother was alive, she'd been certain the queen would have saved her from an arranged marriage. But her mother was dead. And the only remaining soul who knew of her vow was the disturbed and drenched priest standing before her.

"I know," Fr. Gerebran said. "I know, dear girl."

She closed her eyes and swallowed hard. She felt as if the very hounds of hell were closing in about her, as if the little lifeboat she'd been floating in for months had begun taking on water and soon she would be drowning. Tears formed in her eyes and dripped to her chin. Her very bones shook with rage.

Fr. Gerebran's feet padded across the floor, and a moment later, one of his palms cupped her face, his gesture imparting all the tenderness and chastity that her true father lacked. "I don't intend to let him have you," he said. His voice was steel-edged. "I intend to take you away from here. Somewhere safe, where you can live your faith and your vow without persecution. But we must leave swiftly—tonight. Can you make yourself ready?"

She swallowed back her tears and met his eyes and a determined fire rid the water from her lungs. "Yes," she said. "At once."

* * *

"Show me the sign of your favor that my foes may see to their shame, that you console me and give me your help." Fr. Gerebran finishes the psalm, and she joins him in crossing herself.

She prays this last line with fervor. Though their journey has not been an easy one, it already has been marked by substantial providence—and she prays that it will continue to be so. Making it out of Ireland has already been a miracle. But still, she does not feel safe. Not until they are further away from the sea her father's ships may sail and have reached a place they can call home.

Her father is a stubborn man. Relentless. And she knows he will not rest until he gets her back. She knows he won't let her slip from his grasp. Not easily. Not while she may still be found.

As they close their prayer books, Fr. Gerebran traces a cross on her forehead with his sweet-smelling thumb and looks at her with a sad, tired smile.

"Tomorrow will be easier," he says. "You held up admirably today. Now, get some rest."

When he is almost to the door, she croaks, "You'll make sure no one—"

She doesn't know how to finish that sentence. For she isn't really sure what she expects anyone to do. To seize them in the night and drag them back to Oriel? To rob them of their remaining coin and gold they smuggled from the castle? To slit their throats and steal their horse?

A thousand dangers might have befallen them on the road so far, and yet they had not. But a sense of wariness, of suspicion, plagues her each time she thinks about relaxing into sleep. Nightmares stalk at the edges of her mind, ready to spring once she is alone.

But Father seems to know what she means all the same. "Upon my life, princess," he says.

He shuts the door behind him and she is alone. She climbs under the quilts of the bed, and her aching bones sink into the hay pallet. It is a lucky thing she doesn't have to share this bed with another lady traveler. Taking a bed alone at an inn is a rarity, and she doesn't know if she has her supposed pregnancy to thank or sheer providence—but likely both.

For weeks they have been shoved below deck on a creaking ship or flitting between crowded inns. Their only time of solitude has been on the road. Her times without Fr. Gerebran nearby are rarer still, and it is now that her loneliness falls upon her like a heavy shroud.

In quiet moments like these, the grief revisits, slithering upon her like the inevitable chill of winter. She hugs her arms around herself, tears threatening. And she knows it is foolish, but she feels so small. Nothing more than a little girl, lost without her mother, swallowed by the vastness of a world wider and more daunting than she'd ever realized. Friendless, foreign, hunted, in a place that feels and looks nothing like home.

She has no title, no reputation, nothing to ground her, nothing familiar to cling to but her one companion on the road. And the enormity of all she has lost this year nearly crushes the air from her lungs.

There must be some divine hand in it all—there *must* be. But the knowledge does not erase the fear, or the grief, or make her eager to commit to another grueling day on the road, going somewhere yet unseen.

Maybe if she was fleeing *to* somewhere instead of just *from*, this would all feel easier.

They have enough gold with them to live comfortably for a year or more—plus the necessary dowry for her to enter a convent as a postulant, should they find a suitable place. Even then, there is still enough. Throughout their journey, Father has asked her what she would do in this strange new land. He keeps asking her to dream so that she might forget about what came before. But lately she has been too weary to dream.

Tonight is no exception.

She longs for rolling hills, her castle, the friends she's left behind. She longs for her mother, for the chapel she'll never see again, for a father who protects her and whom she needs no protection *from*. She longs for the regularity of her abandoned life: the lessons with Fr. Gerebran, her daily horseback rides, her and her mother's regular trips to the sea. She longs for a time when things made sense.

But it all has vanished over the edge of the horizon, and what lies before her now rests only in the mind of God. She wants to believe that what comes next will be even a fraction as rich and satisfying as what she's left behind, but to hope for such feels premature, gluttonous, naive.

Jesus, she prays once again. *What would you have me do?*

There is only the wind and rain for an answer.

* * *

She wakes with a gasp after dawn.

Vestiges of the nightmare slink away, but always it is the same. Grabbing hands. Running in the dark. Winding mazes and dead ends. Flashes of swords and bursts of fire. The cries of goats and the smell of blood.

She takes a moment to remind herself that she is safe. Whole. And soon they will be even further from Oriel.

She says her morning offering, dresses, ties up her bag to prepare for their travel, and, with some reluctance, slips her prayer book and spare dress under the top layer of her dress, fastening them there to complete the disguise she'd worn last night.

When she arrives downstairs in the cramped kitchen, Fr. Gerebran is already eating a warm breakfast and chatting with the innkeeper's wife in the language of this land. So far they are alone.

The innkeeper's wife's face lights up with apparent fondness as she enters. Fr. Gerebran greets the princess with a nod. The innkeeper's wife gestures toward the bowl before the priest and asks something.

Father, who knows half a dozen languages, has acted as a constant translator for the princess since their departure from Oriel, but this question is simple enough to decipher.

The princess smiles and nods in thanks. A moment later, a bowl of something like porridge is pushed before her, and she sits at the table, says her prayer of thanks, and eats.

Outside there is no sound of rain, but through the open window she can smell the dampness and mud of the street, the light filtering in grey and misty. The innkeeper's wife disappears through a doorway, and soon the only sound is their scraping spoons and the crackle of the hearth.

Fr. Gerebran turns to her. "Our hostess tells me that there is a small town about a two days' journey from here—Geel. It would perhaps be a good place to settle."

"Settle?" the word comes tentatively to her lips. After so long on the road it seems surreal to think about a place to *stay*.

"There is a convent not far from there," Father continues. A smile flicks automatically to her lips at the thought. "And it is a town small enough to be overlooked by anyone seeking us from Oriel, but large enough that we don't have to own land to make our way there. I should at least like to make the acquaintance of the nearby bishop."

She nods and considers his words as she rubs some of the sleep from her eyes. She likes the idea of visiting the convent and meeting the sisters there. And a small town feels far less overwhelming than a city. Her heart still belongs to the countryside, after all.

"What do you think?" he prompts.

"Geel," she turns the name over in her mouth. "It sounds as good a place as any."

Something clangs behind the nearest door, as if a mess of cookery has crashed to the floor. She jumps in spite of herself and looks at Father who meets her gaze with raised eyebrows.

There is yelling, again in the language she does not know, and every nerve in her spine sings of flight.

Is it him? The thought rises automatically to her mind and her heart beats double-time. *Is this where he finally catches them?*

Fr. Gerebran, also half-risen from his seat, tilts his head toward the door, as if straining to decipher the words. Next comes a cry and a shushing sound, and suddenly, the innkeeper's wife appears. She crosses the floor to Father and takes his hand, her eyes wild and desperate and pulls the priest toward the door where the sound of sobbing rises.

"What's happening?" the princess asks, looking between the innkeeper's wife and Father.

"It's the woman I anointed last night," Father explains, "She's not well—"

The princess follows them into a small storage room. A low pallet is laid on the floor—a makeshift sickbed. On it, an elderly woman shivers and shakes. The innkeeper is behind her, trying to hold and shush her, but still the woman sobs, a litany of distressed words tumbling from her mouth. A ceramic bowl lay shattered on the floor, beside the contents of an overturned chamber pot.

The stench is potent. The woman's screams rise in pitch. Father is speaking to the innkeeper, but mid-sentence he switches to Oriel's tongue and says, "Please, can you fetch my anointing oils from my bag at our table? I told them I am no doctor, but I'll do what—"

The old woman's gaze meets hers and the princess sees a panic on her wrinkled face, and a confusion and a hurt like an injured fledgling lying beneath its nest. She doesn't intend to be disobedient, but a compulsion, an instinct, more than a rebellion compels her to step toward the woman.

Before she knows it, the princess is sitting on the edge of the pallet, her hand placed on the twisted quilt between them. The woman does not shrink away from her, but instead looks at her with wary and watery eyes. Her mouth hangs open, but only ragged breaths come out. For now, at least, she has stopped screaming.

The innkeeper mutters something, and Fr. Gerebran translates, "She is prone to confusion and bursts of anger. She sometimes wakes with these fits not knowing who or where she is. She forgets even her own children. The fever has only made it worse."

The innkeeper makes a half-hearted gesture as if to drag the princess away from his mother and return her to her place by the door, but still, she stays.

"—she is prone to violence—" Father continues, now translating for the innkeeper's wife.

But that does not dissuade the princess from reaching out and taking the old woman's hand in her own and running her thumb across the woman's knuckles, her skin as dry as parchment.

"There's no need to be afraid," the princess says. She knows the woman likely cannot understand her—for no one seems to speak her mother tongue here. But she says it nonetheless, hoping her tone can convey what her words cannot. "My name is Dymphna, and I am a friend. You are safe here. And the God of peace desires your healing and wholeness. For he can restore all things."

Though the woman's breaths are still quick as a startled hare's, she has stopped struggling and is now looking at Dymphna with a tentative curiosity. Dymphna squeezes her hand and begins to hum.

It is an old hymn, one her mother taught her. It used to be a favorite of hers whenever she was afraid at night, whether of storms, or nightmares, or scoldings from her father. This was the hymn that always gave her comfort when she was small and afraid. So she hums it now and as she hums, she prays, asking Jesus to restore the woman's peace and mind.

A moment later, the woman's breaths have slowed and the innkeeper lays her back down. He looks between Dymphna and Fr. Gerebran, and murmurs something in amazement. Slow tears leak from his eyes.

* * *

Fr. Gerebran leads their horse by the reins through the muddy streets, one hand hitching up the hem of his cassock to avoid the worst of the slop. The houses ebb away and the road reaches forward into the wilderness beyond, wide and deep.

Now that they have left the inn behind, Dymphna feels a little foolish sitting astride the horse, fake belly still stretching the fabric of her dress. She can't help but think of the Holy Virgin on her way to Bethlehem. For after all, she too is a young virgin, and yet seemingly with child. But she has Fr. Gerebran for her Joseph, and she is carrying the Christ child not in her womb, but in her heart.

She fishes under her dress, and pulls her belongings from underneath and repacks them into their saddlebag.

When they are almost out of town, Fr. Gerebran turns to her, a bemused look in his eye. "Do you know," he asks, "that the fever left her as soon as you prayed?"

No. She hadn't known. But she smiles. It seems that God has chosen to use her here, in this strange land, among these strange people, and she is grateful. Grateful that she can give something back, and repay kindness for kindness.

"Praise God," she says simply.

"They were telling me," Father says, "that the nearest doctor is quite a ways from here. They were beginning to worry that she would die, for her fever has been raging for days and her mind has been weak for longer still. But I think our Lord has restored her of even that."

Up ahead, the sun breaks through the clouds and shines warm and yellow upon the greening fields. A lightness works its way into Dymphna's chest, and she takes a deep breath, feeling her lungs inflate to their fullest and her spirit lift.

What awaits them in Geel? What will their lives look like, a week, even a month from now?

It warms her to think that He has brought her here for some purpose and some necessity, even if she knows not what. All of her life, until now, she had a name that was recognized, a status, a role.

But in this foreign land, she is no one...but that also means she might become *anyone.*

For the first time, the thought excites her rather than frightens her, and the possibilities unfold before her like the wide and weathered road.

They travel in silence for a good while, until the idea comes upon her swift and sudden, as if on the wings of a dove. "Perhaps we could start a hospital," she says. "In Geel. So their sick have somewhere to go. We have plenty of funds, do we not?"

Fr. Gerebran looks back at her and grins. "I like the way you think," he says. "But my dear Dymphna, your heart is made of something purer than any gold we brought from Oriel."

She smiles at his praise and closes her eyes as a ray of sun washes over her. And she is certain now, that whatever becomes of them, no matter where they go, or whether their plans are realized—she is certain that no matter what happens next—it will be good.

* * *

Dymphna and Fr. Gerebran did make it to Geel (modern-day Gheel in Belgium) and used their funds to open a hospital. For some time they lived in peace, until Dymphna's father, Damon, tracked them down. He demanded Dymphna return to Ireland with him as his bride upon pain of death. She steadfastly refused. Though Fr. Gerebran died protecting Dymphna, Damon still succeeded in martyring them both. St. Dymphna & St. Gerebran's tombs still reside in Gheel. There have been many miracles attributed to their relics and intercession. They are patron saints of the mentally ill and fever victims. Their shared feast day is May 15th.

Story 4

Anesthetize

Ben Stapleton

Beware the promises the Emperor lends
Every wish made, the Sultan bends
He comes clad in bones and ragged, rotten clothes
Three days and three nights through the Emperor's sand
The wanderer shall find Solomon's Stone at hand
Should by that Desert King you be cursed
Those wounds only by Solomon's Stone be reversed

The sun's gaze never wavered, never blinked. Its heat seared the marketplace where the roiling crowd ebbed and flowed. The stench of sweat mixed with incense was enough to make Tian gag. Bodies pressed around him. The din of conversations mingled, no one thread he could follow but no demands on him either. Merchants hocked wares to passersby. A farmer barked orders at the farmhands that pulled his grain-laden cart. The obscene mass of humanity should make anyone claustrophobic, but Tian found it liberating. Normal life for him was being stuffed into regal garments and paraded about court. Today he had forgone his usual regal robes for a simpler tunic, kilt, and cloak. The dress of a traveller.

It was unusual for Tian to be out in the market at this time of day. Normally, his bender would wait until later, once he escaped his handlers. Today he wouldn't be prowling the streets for one vice or another. Today he'd given his guards the slip to search for a children's tale. One he hoped would free him from the Emperor's Curse. Wouldn't be the first time he was irresponsible as the prince-heir of Hyades, he'd not been present to his duties and responsibilities for years.

He squeezed his eyes shut and recalled the treasurer rousing him from a drunken stupor to sign tax laws in his father's stead. The captain of his personal guard pounding on an inn where he'd passed out after carousing. Drinking Scorpion's Bite when he should have been lending a careful ear to petitioners in his father's stead. Why his father trusted Tian with anything of late was a wonder. But he was hopeful a break from what life had been could change that.

A flicker of movement caught Tian's eye. Sunlight glinted off metal. He stopped and turned, pulling his hood further up over his head. There was no bright flashing steel among the crowd. So not the guards, but there was another pursuer that worried him more. Tian scanned the shadows between brick buildings and linen awnings, but no sign of the Emperor. A body bumped into Tian. Linen scraped over his bandaged lesions.

"Move out of the way, disease-riddled parasite!" a gruff voice called. Somebody shoved Tian from behind. Pain spread down his back where muscles spasmed as the sores that covered his body flared. He tripped, fell, and cracked his head against a rough clay wall. Blood trickled from a split in his scalp. Spit landed on his shoulder and the heckler, if it was the same man, laughed. Tian swallowed his pride and leaned against the wall. To confront would attract attention, and to attract attention would bring his human pursuers, or worse. Tian drew a jar of a dark green liquid from his pack and took a deep pull. The Scorpion's Bite went down like mud. Its acrid scent burned his nostrils and its acid sting numbed his tongue. After a few moments the numbness spread to his limbs and senses. Blues became gray, reds became rust. But the burning sores calmed to a dull throb keeping time with his heartbeat.

A hand tugged at the corner of Tian's cloak. He glanced down and saw a beggar. A woman whose smile was riddled with holes looked up at him. Her breath carried the stench of the Scorpion, though the scent may have been from his own breath. She extended a gnarled hand towards him. In a mumbling voice, "Can you spare any alms for the poor?"

Tian recoiled, snatched his cloak from her hands and took a few fitful steps back. "I have none to give."

"Why won't you help me?" she pleaded.

Tian shook his head again and shouted, "I've nothing to give!"

"The prince has nothing to give?" The voice was not the woman's. It sounded like beetles crawling over tile. The beggar's deep tanned skin darkened and stretched, her already gaunt form grew thinner. Blue-grey cloak morphed to a patina-covered bronze breastplate. Her face boiled and blurred, and a skull-covered void greeted Tian. Eyes deep as the black of sleep. Dry laughter escaped decayed lips. The Emperor raised one desiccated hand, skeletal phalanges stretched towards Tian.

Tian danced out of reach of the bony fingers and ran into the crowd. He shoved a family aside; the father hurled insults at his back. Legs pumped and lungs burned as Tian sprinted away, hoping the crowd would swallow him and keep him safe in its embrace. Tian skidded around a corner and went sprawling as he tripped over a young man, little older than a boy. He was reed-thin with clothes that hung from his frame like curtains from a drying line. Tian picked himself up, dusted himself off and muttered an apology.

"That's quite alright. What's got you so spooked anyways?" The man glanced over Tian's shoulder and frowned. His eyes darted from dark alleyways to shadows under stoops and awnings.

"I, uh," Tian stammered. The fellow probably wouldn't believe him if he told the truth anyways. "Saw a ghost." Tian glanced over his shoulder. An ivory skull peeked through the bustling crowd. Bodies passed before it and the Emperor was another ten feet closer without having taken a step.

"You've seen him too?" The man followed Tian's eyes.

Shocked, Tian replied, "I thought I was the only one."

"Where do you think the faerie stories come from? We'd best be off before he can catch us." He turned and ran down the street, away from the Emperor.

"No lesions," Tian muttered to himself as he studied the fellow's retreating form. Tian followed after, and between panted breaths he asked, "So you know the fables of Solomon's Stone?"

"Aye, though I'm not so certain they're fables. Whether or not they are, don't have much to lose at this point. You know it's rude not to introduce yourself. You can call me Mark." Mark coughed, a nasty wet sound.

"You can call me Tian." Tian furrowed his brow and glanced at Mark. "Are you alright?"

"Never better," Mark muttered around phlegmy lips then gave a wry chuckle. "You've the same name as the prince? Wish you could have brought some of his palanquin bearers with you."

The sores first appeared three years ago. Tian woke in one of his usual haunts, a house of ill-repute. The light streaming in through curtains was blinding. Sunken among silken sheets, he didn't know if he'd spent his night alone or not. The last thing he recalled was downing shots of liquor and wrapping his fists for the ring. The adrenaline suffused his veins as the crowd screamed for violence. Who was it he'd been pitted against? Some poorly trained gladiator, no doubt. A flicker in his memory of a man with brown hair, speech slurred by a broken jaw, begging for his life. Most of Tian's opponents were poor sports, they'd never let the crown prince be in any real danger. Not after what happened to his brother Julian.

Tian's head pounded as he sat forward and his stomach

wrenched. Whether from jabs or drinks he didn't know, though the headache was more likely from the latter. His vision swam as he examined his hands. A little bit of dried blood caked Tian's knuckles. Maybe he had gone all the way this bout. He granted clemency for most, the games were mere physical contests after all. But if he'd been deep enough in his cups he couldn't be sure how far he'd gone. Tian groped the bedside table for a bottle. Clumsy fingers closed around the neck, and he flicked the cork off with his thumb. The burn of alcohol scratched his throat, and he hoped the fire would cleanse his mind.

Getting up, Tian stretched and took in the room. It had stone walls, decorated with paintings of men and women at leisure. Aside from the bed and a few tables the room was bare, not even a trunk or dresser. He must have gone for a binge after yesterday's bout, then. There was a door leading out to a hallway and another leading to a washroom. Tian washed up and dried himself using the soft towels provided. That was when he noticed a rusty brown speck on his thigh. He brushed it off with the back of his hand and smeared blood across his leg. Blood thundered in Tian's ears when he saw the sanguine liquid ooze from the opening. It could just be a knick from the bout, right? Tian poked and prodded the hole in his skin. Its edges weren't jagged like the wounds he'd suffered before. It was too smooth. He had seen a wound like this once before, or several of them. Julian's wounds.

With shaking hands, Tian threw his clothes back on, hoping the blood wouldn't stain through before he returned to the palace. He snatched his bottle off the table and sprinted through the house, ignoring the servants that called after him in surprise.

Tian only stopped when he reached the alleyway outside. Breath heavy and quick, he tentatively lifted the hem of his kilt. The blood flow hadn't been stemmed at all, and looking closer he saw other sores forming on his skin. He blanched and turned pale, stomach threatening to heave up whatever delicacies he'd enjoyed the previous night. It was just like Julian's condition. He took another swallow of alcohol and jumped when the skull-crowned figure of the Emperor beckoned from the shadows across the alley. Tian froze at the appearance of that malignant spirit. Despite years of seeing this monster at the corners of his vision, all the way back to Julian's final days, Tian never grew used to it. But there was a part of him that found the Emperor alluring. As if the layers of cracked skin and rotting flesh held a secret Tian could unpeel if he but just spent enough time dissecting.

You want to forget, a sandpaper voice spoke.

"I don't want to suffer as Julian did," Tian pleaded. The empty eye sockets of the Emperor's skull beckoned Tian. He stared into those voids and was awash in memory. Holding the knife in the coliseum, a young man with brown hair and amber eyes stared up at Tian. His mouth repeated the same words, though Tian didn't hear them, *Spare me! Spare me! Spare me!* The longer he looked, he saw another pleading. Other words washed over his ears. The roar of the crowd mingled with the sound of rushing water. In the memory, a leathery hand grasped Tian's forearm and guided the blade to the defeated man's throat. Steel flashed and red ran.

The Desert King laughed, producing from beneath his moth-eaten robes a jar of some dark green liquid. *Take and drink.* He exaggerated the length of each word. Cooing like a mother coaxing her child to eat, *Forget.* The Desert King thrust the jar into Tian's outstretched hands.

The dark green liquid tasted like honey at first, but an aftertaste of bile stuck in the back of Tian's mouth. The Emperor had heard his deepest desires before. Why shouldn't this be any different?

The rising moonlight illuminated the desert around Mark and Tian. An eerie pale glow that set the orange landscape in a blue-tinged grayscale. A dusty wind had picked up, the sand carried aloft. It was little more than a nuisance now, the grains piling up on their clothes or in their packs. Still, they crouched behind the shelter of a small rock outcropping that broke the wind. The previous two days had been spent in silence, neither wanting to waste more water than they had to. With the curtain of night drawn, they were willing to break their taciturn agreement.

"Where do you suppose the Stone is?" Tian asked.

"I'm not certain we can find it on a map. The fable goes, 'three days and three nights through the Emperor's sands,'" Mark quoted. "I think we just need to survive three days' travel."

"Another day in the heat and I'll shrivel to death. What makes you sure?"

"Trusting reason alone has helped me little." Mark coughed into the back of his hand.

"What else is there?"

"Do you remember when you first met the Emperor?"

"I do," Tian answered, a lump in his throat.

"All his glorious pestilence, all his alluring decay. I don't know what he offered you, but he offered me what I thought were truths." Mark stopped and stared at the horizon. His eyes glistened, the reflected moon wavered in his pupils. "Knowledge to sate my curiosity. But it wasn't just the promise of knowledge that enticed me, it was living out something that wasn't for me."

Tian knew the allure of living another's life. "What was that for you?"

"I was born to farmers along the river." A sombre tone entered his voice. "My folks wanted to send me to collegium but could not afford it. We struck a deal with a local glassblower. I would apprentice under him for five years and in exchange he would sponsor my education." Mark paused then and gazed up at the veil of stars. The growing wind stalled a moment. "I just wanted to get there faster. So I took a different offer. Wound up with a scholarship when another child died of plague. Three years after that, my parents met their own end. Home burned down. They'd become trapped." Mark's voice caught and his shoulders shook.

Tian had no words to offer; he reached out and embraced the young man. He pulled back and the two laid back to gaze up at the stars. An hour passed before either spoke again. "You might have died in that fire, too," Tian said as he plucked the strings to his haversack.

Mark shook his head. "I spent months researching what I could of the Emperor, neglected my studies even. I might have died or might have saved them, but either way the guilt was eating me from the inside. Did the Emperor return to you with later offers?"

Tian nodded.

"He did the same for me, promises of power or love. Distractions to hide behind. But what really bothers me is that boy whose place I took. Sometimes I can't help but think I caused his sickness."

"It was similar for me. My brother. He had a—a fall," Tian choked out. "Just as I thought how frail he was and how much better it would be for me to inherit our family's fortune. It isn't like I pushed him..." Tian trailed off, and he took another swig of Bite.

"You still drink that stuff?" Mark asked, nodding to the Bite.

"Helps dull the pain. Up here," Tian pointed to his head, then at his bare arms, where the sores' pus glinted under the lunar glow, "and here."

Mark shook his head. "I dumped mine out when I decided to come out here. Lightened the pack, and I figured I should leave anything the Emperor gave me, otherwise what's the point in finding the Stone?"

Tian opened his mouth and shut it. "Huh, I figured the Stone would heal this affliction."

"The legends I read were unclear. In some, the Emperor 'gifted' those he cursed with ailments, though I've no rashes or lesions." Mark coughed. And coughed. And coughed. His body convulsed with each heave. He pulled a white handkerchief from his bag and wiped something from his mouth. Tian saw a dark spot on the cloth. "Other tales don't mention an illness, just supplicants leaving with a mind broken and returning with one mended."

The wind stiffened and tore at their clothes. The steady drift before became more insistent. Grains were driven into Tian's sores. He cried out. Mark leapt to his feet and pointed at the horizon, where the moon backlit a hunched figure.

"Who do you think that is?" Tian asked, his tongue like cotton and not just for want of water.

"Could be a wandering trader," Mark said. "I've heard they sometimes travel at night to avoid the heat of the day."

The newcomer had an odd gait, taking a few strides here and there before stopping. Then it turned and scuttled to the side. The gusts grew stronger. Tore at Mark and Tian's clothes like it wanted to pull them towards the figure on the dune. They pulled scarves across their mouths and noses to keep their mouths from filling with sand. The stars and moon dimmed as more and more particles filled the air.

"Whoever this is doesn't seem right," Tian remarked. A dull throb gnawed at Tian's flesh, pumping in time with his heart. His vision swam and the sand bored further into his wounds. Tian took a drink of Bite, sighing as the sweet familiar sludge ran down his throat.

Mark shouted something over the howling wind, though Tian couldn't hear him. They should just let this fellow join their makeshift camp, if camp it could be called without tent nor bedroll. The figure drew closer. What was there to worry about? The fellow seemed normal enough, dressed in his dark green breastplate and robes ripped to shreds. Something was shaking Tian's shoulder, a violent and urgent motion. At last Tian heard the shouts, "It's the Emperor! Run, fool!"

Tian yelped and stumbled away from their rocky bivouac, deeper into the desert. The Bite worked its magic, and he felt he could run like when he was a child. The Desert King took crooked steps to follow, dried ligaments and tendons creaking over the growing storm with an unnatural volume. Tian sprinted faster. He didn't stop until the aches returned, when the Bite wore off. Breathing heavy and coughing sand, he risked a glance back. Their footprints were lost, swallowed by the wind-driven sand.

Low laughter like gravel chased them.

* * *

It was a sunny day when Tian and Julian were allowed to play in the garden. Bright green leaves covered the landscape, interrupted by yellows and reds and whites of flowers. Their father was always strict about not letting them roam free, so they had two guards keeping a close eye on them. Julian was older than Tian by a few years. Despite this, Julian was shorter by a head. His skin was a pallid color, his eyes sunken. And he bled easily. Once, he'd tripped and skinned his knee on a rock. Instead of cuts that ran like plowed furrows, his skin had torn completely, like gift paper from a present. But the sores were the worst. Poultices concocted by the royal alchemists and apothecaries yielded no substantial change, aside from slowing the bleeding when Julian's wounds wept. A "blood weakness" the physicians had called it. They shook their heads like nothing could be done. Somehow Julian hadn't lost his excitement for adventure.

"Let's go swimming!" Julian exclaimed, trying to keep his voice hushed so the guards couldn't hear their plotting.

"Are you up for it?" Tian whispered back.

"Never been healthier."

"I'll lose the guards then meet you at the pool." Tian scampered into the garden. The guards shouted and chased after him. They wouldn't expect the invalid to wander off on his own. Tian sprinted down a bank, careened around thorn bushes and dove under a fern. Two leather boots paused for a moment a few yards from where he crouched. Tian held his breath, face turning beet red. The boots clambered off further into the garden, and away from the pool. He let his breath out slowly, and crept from under the fronds. A furtive glance about showed the guards nowhere near, and he scampered back to where he'd left Julian.

The path was empty, and faint sounds of splashing echoed from the pool below. With a laugh on his lips, Tian sprinted down the hill to the bank of the pool. Its water was a crisp and clear cerulean, little flecks of jovial sunlight reflecting off the ripples in the water. On the far side the water turned white as it cascaded down the cliff and deeper into the palace. In the middle of the pool Julian swam, arms whirling in arcs and legs kicking. His face was split in a grin of pure joy, the kind he hadn't worn for years. Tian giggled, too. Everybody else saw the sickly heir to the throne, and tried to protect him, but he couldn't live in a bubble of safety.

Tian dove into the cool water. On land, he was the better athlete. Always able to run faster, jump more freely, not be afraid of taking a tumble. But in the water, Julian could shine. Tian broke through the surface of the water where the warm air kissed his face. He heard Julian laughing, a high pitched shriek like when a child thinks he was getting away with mischief.

It really was a shame, his brother's condition. Even as a child, Julian was generous and caring as a prince ought to be. Perhaps a bit brash, but what great leader could there be who wasn't a little bold? But deep in Tian's stomach he felt Julian would never make a great prince. Too frail and weak. If only their father would pass the inheritance to Tian, then Tian could have Julian as an advisor. And Julian could swim all he wanted. More peals of laughter wafted over the water to Tian. He swiveled his head to search for his brother, but Julian was nowhere to be found. What Tian had mistaken for sounds of joy were screams of terror.

Heart rattling in his ribcage, Tian paddled for the top of the waterfall. He hauled himself onto a rock and peered about the pool. Four rocks down, Julian was caught. The water rushed over his head. Every few seconds he'd wrestle free and gasp for air or scream before being shoved back under. Tian leapt from his stone, feet slipping on the water-coated surface. Julian went under again, his thrashing growing more urgent.

"Your Highness!" a stern voice called from the shore, the guards returning from their snipe hunt. "Stay away from the waterfall, it's dangerous!"

"Where is your brother?" the other guard's voice called.

Tian landed on the next rock. Julian broke through the water again, a shout on his lips. One of the guards rushed to the water's edge, tossing his armor aside. Bracing for another jump, Tian's foot caught on a divot. He stumbled and nearly fell into the water. Julian's thrashing had done a little to free him from the vice that held him, but the water shoved his body closer to the steep drop. Tian jumped.

This time, he hadn't had the time to balance and skinned his knee on the rough stone. A sharp sting dug at his knee. Hot blood trickled out. The guard tossed his weapon aside and dove into the water, paddling hard to reach the boys. Julian was forced under the water again, only this time he didn't bob back up.

Tian crouched, ready to leap again. A horrifying face stared up from the murky shadow cast into the water. A face of sunken eyes and rotting flesh. *You can take the throne, you know. Wouldn't have to protect this sickly thing.*

Tian froze.

Julian surfaced one last time screaming, "Help me Ti—" before he jolted loose from the rocks that held him. He tumbled over the cataract. Tian screamed as the guard reached him and pulled him from the rock's edge. A cackle like snake rattles split the air.

A boiling red sun, swollen and gorged, set over the dune before Mark and Tian. Its sweltering heat squeezed what little water they had left from their pores. Red rays of light streamed down into the next valley, illuminating a pure white stone that sat at the bottom.

"Solomon's Stone," Tian said in awe. Its great mass rose nearly to the rim of the bowl of sand. Faces smooth and polished, white surfaces unmarred by any specks of dust. It twinkled in the sun, splitting the light into a kaleidoscope of dazzling colors. The wind grew stronger. The dust thickened in the air. Mark and Tian had not stopped to rest since that second night when the Emperor found them.

"The third day," Mark breathed, his voice muffled by the cloth drawn over his nose and mouth.

What once was clandestine evil to that uncanny wind that dogged their journey now left no doubt that it was bent on halting their progress. A veritable wall of sand billowed up from all around, barreling towards Mark and Tian. They stumbled down the steep sides of the dune, slipping as loose sand gave way beneath their weight. The wall of debris rushed ever onwards, and the sands around their feet rattled and boiled like thousands of snakes burrowed beneath its surface. The shifting sand revealed skeletal hands reaching out from the ground towards the stone.

"Do you see them?" Tian shouted over the rushing wind. Whatever reply Mark spoke was caught up and borne away. They struggled on. The storm was now a vortex swirling about them, centered on Solomon's Stone. Something caught Tian's sandal, and he collapsed. Sand pressed into the raw flesh where his sandal straps tore his skin. He glanced down and saw hands of ivory twisting around his ankle. The wind uncovered more of the skeletons that ringed the little valley, cadavers rising from the earth. The dead that failed to reach Solomon's Stone. Another pair of hands clasped onto his thigh. The bodies pressed around Tian, and a shadow fell across the sun. He reached out but recoiled when he saw it was not Mark but the Desert King who stood before him. The creature's outstretched hand offered no help, only a jar of the Bite.

Tian mustered the last of his strength and smashed the jar in the Emperor's hand. The clay shattered, and its contents hissed and sputtered when it touched the ground. Where it met Tian's skin it burned, and where it entered his lesions, it seared his flesh. Tian screamed. The Desert King withdrew, stepping through the curtain of dust that was the storm's constricting eye. And another shadow passed before Tian. Mark's hand grasped Tian's and pulled him free. Together they scrambled and crawled to the brilliant white stone. They reached with trembling fingers and brushed its too smooth surface. All went dark.

. . .

What may have been hours or days later, Tian blinked his eyes against the blinding sun. Two vultures wheeled far above him. The sky was clear, no sand lacerated his skin. The only sign of the sandstorm was his shredded clothes and slices criss-crossed over his body. Dim memories floated across his subconscious. Images of him leaping the last stone to save Julian. In some he slipped when landing and plunged to his own death. In others he kept his feet and pulled Julian to safety. Even in those visions, his brother passed within the year as his condition grew worse. The vultures circled lower. Tears streamed down Tian's face, and he longed to reach for a jar of Bite.

Then Mark was kneeling at Tian's side, pouring water between his lips. Mark offered a hand, weak but steady, and hauled Tian to his feet. The younger man's eyes were haunted. A sole pinprick of light flickered behind them, like a reflection of Solomon's Stone deep in the man's soul. Tian and Mark embraced. They climbed out of the bowl between dunes where Solomon's Stone had been, though there was no sign of the alabaster rock.

"I suppose we've got to find our way back now." Mark's voice was thin and warm, like a single thread of wool.

"And what do we do once we've returned?"

Mark shrugged, "Live, I suppose. The way we didn't before."

Tian considered his open palm. "Easier said than done. The Stone helped, but I still feel the desire." He closed his hand and opened it again, "I'm not sure how long I can hold onto that assurance."

"We'll have to remind each other on occasion." Mark flashed a toothy smile. "Besides, I'd want to keep in touch with the Crown Prince. Lots of opportunity for sponsored studies with your pockets."

Tian reeled. "How-how did you?"

Mark roared and doubled over, his stomach heaving as tears streaked down his face. "You really thought I wouldn't figure out you're the Crown Prince!? Same name; roughly the same age, though the Bite ages you; and he's been rumored to have a skin condition. Doesn't take a scholar."

Tian continued stammering protestations, which only drove the bemused Mark into further fits.

Mark clapped Tian's shoulder. "Don't worry, I won't hold any of this over your head. We've both been through the same shit. Saw the same demons."

The return journey stretched before them, and behind stretched shadows. The two vultures followed their every step back over the dunes, but they never grew closer than far-off black flecks in the sky. Mark and Tian passed the hours sharing what they would do once they got back, most of it just wistful thinking. Only a pale phantom of the false king they'd once relied on shimmered at the corners of their visions. Upon their return, tales spread of the Prince and his royal advisor. Tian's skin never fully healed from those sores. In time, though, they faded from the angry red they had been.

Nor did the Desert King's whispers ever leave the periphery of their thoughts, but they were no longer alone in a prison of their own minds with his call.

Story 5

When the Lights Touch the Earth

Madeline Shepley

"I can't believe we're finally here!"

Anastasia came to a halt several yards from their gate at the sound of her daughter's voice. She watched as Lily, golden-brown braid swaying as she walked, took in the rustic scenery of Anchorage's airport. Her own heart clenched as she fiddled with a strand of her own golden-brown hair. She wished she could share Lily's enthusiasm.

I still can't believe she talked me into this, Anastasia thought.

"Mom?" Lily's voice broke through her pensive stupor. "Are you okay?"

Anastasia met her daughter's aurora-green eyes, and her heart clenched again. Lily's eyes were pinched with concern. Then, she walked back over to her mother. She took one of her mother's hands and squeezed it.

"Don't worry. Dad would want us to have fun. He'd be proud of me–proud of us–for following in his footsteps."

Anastasia managed a grateful smile, though she couldn't seem to get her heart to match her exterior illusion. *As long as we don't follow exactly in his footsteps...I couldn't bear that.* She swallowed, guilt at her pessimism hitting her. *I need to protect Lily...but I can't be overly pragmatic. She's been wanting to do this for over a decade, and she did insist on this trip for her birthday after all...*

She managed to pull herself from her thoughts and take up her suitcase again. She walked past Lily and led her away. "You're right, Lily. Should we get our rental, then?"

Lily nodded, and they set off towards the rental car counter. The man staffing the counter quickly fetched their keys and rental agreement.

As Anastasia signed it, he asked, "Where are you guys driving?"

"We're going up to Fairbanks," Lily said with a smile.

"What are you doing there?"

"We're taking advantage of this year's strong geomagnetic storms to see the northern lights," Anastasia supplied. "My daughter has wanted to since she was little."

"Oh, excellent," he said cheerily. "As long as you're up there for a while, you're bound to get good views. I went there to visit family a few months ago and saw amazing displays." He pointed at a sign near them on the counter listing several road names. "Take note of these prohibited roads. A few of them are near Fairbanks or on the way, so be wary. You wouldn't want to be on one accidentally. Road conditions are often treacherous."

Not unlike the Parks Highway eleven years ago... she mused sadly, but forced a smile onto her face and said out loud, "Thanks for the warning."

"Not a problem!" he replied, handing over the keys. "Safe travels!"

Anastasia nodded slightly, then led Lily away. They found the black SUV they'd been assigned. While loading their luggage in the back, Anastasia noted the car's exterior mirrored her mood.

It's like it knows how much I don't want to make this drive.

But Lily'd been relentlessly insistent. She wanted to retrace her parents' auroral footsteps all the way up the Parks Highway between Anchorage and Fairbanks. Anastasia had protested that flying into

Fairbanks would be easier, but Lily found a *way* cheaper flight to Anchorage and wouldn't be deterred.

"It's Dad telling us he wants us to make this a road trip," she had asserted.

"Honey, your dad *doesn't* speak through flight sales."

"Yes, he *does*," she'd said. "Besides, you can put the hundreds you'll save by flying into Anchorage towards those overpriced college textbooks I have to buy this summer."

Anastasia hadn't been able to help conceding that point and soon found herself booking flights for Lily's upcoming spring break.

"Should we get this show on the road?" Lily asked as Anastasia shut the trunk and they both got into the SUV. Her daughter, smiling slightly, offered a hand.

Anastasia tried to make her smile more natural-looking to not rain on Lily's parade. She took her daughter's hand. "Yes."

If Lily doubted her mom's sincerity, she didn't show it. Instead, she squeezed it gently. "Great. Let's head out!"

Anastasia turned the key in the ignition.

I sure hope I'm ready...

* * *

"Ready to see the northern lights, honey?" came John's excited voice to her left. "In under four hours, we'll be where all the action happens!"

Anastasia beamed at her husband, the excitement in his aurora-green eyes infectious. She leaned over the center console to kiss his cheek. "I was born ready for that—" She made a silly face. "—but *not* for this cold. Hopefully, our winter gear is adequate for the Fairbanks chill."

"Don't worry. I extensively researched the best ways to stay warm in the Last Frontier," he assured her, grin confident. "No Alaskan chill will take my beloved from me." He took up her hand, kissing it.

"Definitely not," she agreed, sitting contentedly back into her seat. "I suppose it isn't even *that* cold. Last I checked, it's only fifteen degrees out."

"See? We're used to that in Chicago!"

Anastasia laughed. "You're right...just not this time of year. Wasn't it fifty degrees when we boarded our flight to Anchorage?"

"Well, it depends on what Mother Nature's mood is. Remember the spring break it was five below?"

"Yeah," she said with a smile. "But I think that worked out for the best. I know my parents wanted to show you around, but I loved getting to drink cocoa and watch movies instead. That was a fun time."

"Yeah," he agreed. "Too bad it wasn't Lily's spring break this year. It would've been nice to bring her. She *really* wanted to come." His face contained wistfulness when he glanced at her, eyes rippling like the ribbons of light gracing the skies of the high northern latitudes. "Man, she begged us so much!"

Anastasia couldn't help the knowing smile tugging at the corners of her lips. Lily had been baffled to not be invited. She'd continually insisted on going, even offering to give away *all* her stuffed animals in exchange. Her begging only grew more determined once she had a taste of the phenomena. When a strong geomagnetic storm had sent undulating colors strolling across the sky on her birthday a few months prior, she couldn't get enough. She'd asserted it was a sign she should go on her parents' trip until her grandparents dropped her parents off at O'Hare.

"Oh yeah," she finally said with a laugh. "She didn't relent until you promised her pictures."

"And I *will* get them for her. As I said to her, 'cross my heart and hope to die.'"

"She'll like that, and it'll hopefully make her less salty with being left at home." Her lips unfurled into a softer smile. "By the way, it was so nice of your parents to watch her on this anniversary trip. I mean, we haven't taken a trip, just us, quite like this since the year after her birth."

"Oh yeah!" he exclaimed, a matching smirk appearing on his lips. "What a great trip. Although, those scorpions were the worst..."

A boisterous laugh tumbled out of Anastasia. "Agreed, but them getting into our tent was *totally* your fault. You left the tent flap unzipped like an amateur."

John started to protest, mock indignation coming over him for her daring to doubt his outdoorsmanship. However, his gaze flicked towards something up ahead and indicated a sign a few tenths of a mile up the road. "There's a gas station ahead."

"Do we need any?"

Her husband glanced at their fuel gauge. "Not sure. I remember hearing gas stations can be sparse on this highway. Where's the next one?"

Anastasia opened GasBuddy to search for the next gas station. "Looks like it's ninety-four miles away."

He eyed their fuel gauge. "I think we can make that."

"Can you check to be sure?"

John nodded and pressed some buttons on the wheel. The display flickered and crackled before showing a range of one hundred fifty miles.

"Does it normally flicker and crackle like that?" She scratched her head.

He shrugged, glancing back at the road. "Not sure, but looks like we have enough fuel. I haven't seen anything like that before. I wonder if it's interference from the geomagnetic storms NOAA forecasted for this week... Geomagnetic storms are known to mess with electronics and satellites."

"Do you think it'd mess with our fuel range?"

He shook his head. "I don't think so. The range's numerical value comes from the fuel tank itself. The storms can't change how much fuel we have left."

"That's a valid point."

He grabbed her hand. "So are you cool with waiting for gas?"

Anastasia flashed him a smile, pushing down a nagging feeling that something was off. "I trust your judgment."

Most of the next hour and a half passed in a flash. They spent the time snacking, admiring the fresh white blanket across the landscape, and chatting about their favorite memories together. Then, a sudden sputtering sound interjected itself in their conversation. The car decelerated and coasted to a stop in the middle of their lane.

"What the heck?" Anastasia muttered. "We have two miles left before the gas station. We should have fifty-six miles left."

"Hmmm..." John peered at the range again. "That's what it says here. I'm not sure what's going on." He pressed the accelerator, but nothing happened. "Looks like we're out of gas."

A pit opened up in her stomach. "We probably should've stopped back there."

John bit his lip and nodded, sorrow entering his eyes before glancing at Anastasia. "I'm sorry, honey. I should've filled up when we had a chance." He flashed a small smile at her, trying to lighten the mood. "Remember when I called you at two in the morning in college because I forgot to fill up before coming home from an away game?"

She couldn't help laughing, rolling her eyes. "You mean the time you woke me up the night before an exam to pick you up twenty minutes outside of town?"

"Yeah. Good thing you already loved me, right?"

Anastasia managed another laugh. "I suppose you're right..." She kissed him. "But real talk. What should we do? We're in the middle of nowhere without gas."

He pursed his lips. "Well, the station should only be about two miles away. I could hike there to get help."

"Are you sure? The roads are covered in snow, and this terrain is mountainous."

After a moment, he replied, "I'll be fine. The station is supposed to be right along this road." He then indicated there were zero bars on his phone. "Besides, we don't have service." He managed a reassuring smile. "If you stay here to wait for the next car to pass by, we'll double our chances of getting help. Sound good?" He saw the apprehension on her face, so he added. "Do you trust me?"

After a moment, she nodded. "With my life."

"Then, I'll get going." He pulled on his coat, hat, and gloves. "We'll be back together in no time. This'll make excellent lore for Lily when we return."

This provoked a laugh out of Anastasia. "Okay, honey. You tell yourself that."

John winked, leaning in to kiss her. "Don't worry. I will."

She kissed him back then he exited the vehicle. As she watched him disappear up the road, she prayed fervently for his safe arrival at the station.

* * *

A few hours after leaving the airport, Anastasia pulled off the Parks Highway into an isolated gas station. Her heart clenched as they coasted in and parked at one of the pumps.

I never thought I would ever *return here...* She stared at the steering wheel, frozen in thought.

"Mom, want me to go pump the gas?" came Lily's voice.

Anastasia's head whipped to face her daughter and shook her head. *No, no, no! I* can't *have history repeat itself!* She scrambled out the door, wallet in hand. "No, Lily," she replied. "You're not pumping the gas. It's snowy and slippery out there. I don't want you getting hurt." She slammed the car door behind her.

The sound of the passenger door echoed behind her before Lily, worry dominating her features, appeared at her side. "Seriously. Let me help you. I can pum—"

"Get back in the car."

"But, Mom..."

Her heart quickened in her chest. *I can't lose her, too.* "Please. Just listen to me."

"Okay, fine," Lily pressed her lips into a thin line of helplessness. "I won't pump the gas. But can I at least use the bathroom? I've been holding it for the past twenty minutes." Discomfort replaced helplessness. "I don't think I can wait much longer."

Anastasia started to argue, but relented. "Fine. Be quick about it, okay?"

Lily nodded, taking off. Anastasia watched her daughter's back until the convenience store's doors swallowed her. *Relax. She's safe for now.* Her trembling hands struggled to fish her credit card out of her wallet. *Come on, Anastasia! What's wrong with you?*

After what felt like forever, she finally managed to pay. While putting the nozzle into the car, her eyes swam in deep pools of tears, blurring her vision. *You can't let this place get to you. You need to get your act together before Lily comes back. She can't see how close you are to falling apart. It'll ruin this trip.* She bit her lip, trying to dry up her eyes with her coat sleeves. *She doesn't deserve that.*

Anastasia watched as the numbers went up at the pump. *Just focus...on the gas, on the numbers. If you don't think about John and how dangerous this place is, you...you'll be fine...* But it was easier said than done, and Anastasia found herself shifting from leg to leg and tapping against the car's body as she waited for the interminable pumping to cease.

Suddenly, the nozzle clicked, shaking her out of the worried introversion infecting her entire being. *That was quick...*

The quiet of the gas station lot hit her.

Wait, where's Lily? She should be back by now. Her heart skipped several beats as she struggled to keep her breathing even. *How could you be so stupid? You should've paid attention! She might be hurt! You need to find her!* Her head swiveled around so much that she almost got vertigo. Her eyes darted around the lot until she spotted her daughter standing still in front of something sticking out of a snowbank on the lot's edge. Her shoulders sagged in relief.

Thank goodness she's okay. Then, she noticed how close she was standing to the road. *But why'd she wander over there? It's not safe.*

Her heart clenched as she dashed over. *She can't do this to me. Not today. Not here!*

"Lily, what the *hell* are you doing?" she shouted as she got within Lily's earshot. "You scared me to death! I can't lose *you*, too!"

Lily didn't answer. She didn't even meet her mother's eyes. Her gaze remained fixed on the snowbank, tears flooding her eyes like spring mountain meltoff.

That stopped Anastasia dead in her tracks.

"Lily?" she asked tentatively, inching forward. "Honey, what's wrong?"

Lily sniffled, pointing wordlessly at a wooden cross stuck in the snowbank. The cross had big, black letters on it in sharpie:

John Hepburn
Beloved Son, Husband, and Father
1980–2014

Anastasia didn't need further invitation to bury her daughter in her embrace.

* * *

A truck finally stopped to help Anastasia a few hours after John left. The driver offered to tow Anastasia's car to the nearest gas station.

"Oh, that'd be great!" she blubbered, relief crashing over her like a giant wave. "My husband left a while ago to get help nearby." She smiled. "It'll be nice to reunite with him."

"I bet." He returned the smile, hooking up towing cables to her car. "You know, I bet he's probably there already, though this snow might be a hindrance." His smile broadened. "If he's not, we'll pick him on the way."

"Perfect!" she replied. Then, they got in his truck and on the road, Anastasia riding shotgun.

After about two minutes, they arrived at the gas station. Red and blue lights danced around the sparse station, reflecting off the snowflakes and the already high snowbank. A couple of police cars and an ambulance crowded what appeared to be a crimson sedan near the lot entrance. Anastasia's eyes widened at the sight. *Hopefully, those involved are okay...*

A police officer saw them attempt to turn in and signaled them to stop. Anastasia rolled down the window. "What's going on, officer?"

"You can't turn in here. We're investigating a fatal accident."

"I'm helping this woman get her car to the nearest gas station," the driver told the cop, indicating the car hitched to the back of his truck. "She and her husband ran out of gas about two miles south on the Parks Highway."

The cop nodded then flicked his gaze back to Anastasia. "Where's your husband?"

"He hiked up this way after we ran out of gas to get help. We didn't see him on the road, so he should be here already since it's not far. Would it be okay if we pulled in, so I can find him? We're not used to mountains in the Midwest. I want to make sure he's okay."

The worry on her face must've made an impression. The police officer's face softened with sympathy. "No problem, ma'am. Pull up by the convenience store and ask around. Just stay clear of the accident scene."

"Yes, sir," she agreed. "Thank you so much."

Once the cop peeled away from their talk, the driver parked the truck where requested. Anastasia hopped out, slipping a bit herself, phone at the ready with a recent photo of John. *Please let him be around here somewhere...I know he can handle a two mile hike.*

However, whether in the convenience store or at the couple of idle cars at the pumps, no one recognized her husband. With each no, the weight of her worry bore down even more, and she couldn't help but steal glances at the accident scene. *Why hasn't anyone seen him? He should've arrived a couple hours ago.*

Out of people to ask, she wandered back to the driver and his truck. He'd graciously agreed to wait until she located John, even offering to fill up Anastasia's car while she searched.

"Any luck yet?" he asked.

Anastasia shook her head, heart pounding faster and faster like it wanted to race right to John's location and be consoled by his embrace. "None. I don't get it. This is the closest gas station, and it's a straight shot. There's no way he could get lost, even in the snow." She scrubbed some snowflakes off her phone screen. "He should be around *somewhere...*"

"Why not ask the police then?"

"Are you sure?" She glanced over at the emergency lights. *I really hope John isn't involved...* "They're still investigating the accident. I don't want to bother them."

"They probably wouldn't mind," he replied reassuringly, following her gaze. "Maybe he was a witness to that accident. The cops are probably questioning him. Then, it'd make sense you haven't seen him yet. The accident looks fairly fresh to me."

Anastasia, starting to sweat despite the chill, managed a grateful smile. "Okay, I'll head over. Thanks for waiting. Sorry for taking forever."

"Don't worry about it." He waved off her apology. "I'd do the same if I were in the same situation with my wife. She'll understand why I'm late home."

She nodded slightly then made her way over to the knot of police and paramedics at the lot's edge. She nearly fell several times due to the icy area. *No wonder there was an accident...*

As she approached, a couple of officers apprehended her. "Ma'am, I told you that you can't be over here," the one from earlier said. "It's the site of an active investigation."

"I know...I'm sorry," she said. "If I could just have a minute more of your time."

"What for?" the other asked.

"As I told your colleague earlier, I'm looking for my husband. I've searched everywhere here. I can't find him. I don't know what else to do…"

"Do you have a picture of him?" the first asked, beckoning her over with a wave and a look of pity.

Anastasia nodded. She showed them a picture on her phone of her family on a recent outing to the Adler Planetarium.

The second officer gulped and glanced at the first. They exchanged a look.

Oh no. Please, God, no. That can't *be good…* she thought, heart stumbling in her chest. "Wh…what's going on, officers?"

"We should've brought you over sooner," the second managed after a pause.

"Why?"

They immediately led her over to the ambulance where paramedics loaded a body bag into it. As they approached, they gestured for the paramedics to stop.

"Ma'am," the first officer said tentatively as the bag was unzipped. "Is this your husband?"

The face the paramedics revealed unleashed a cascade of tears onto Anastasia's face and shattered her entire world.

The whole rest of the ride to Fairbanks, Anastasia and Lily held each other's hands across the center console. A reflective silence settled on them once the tears stopped flowing, not lifting until they reached Fairbanks. Anastasia hadn't pressed her daughter about her feelings, knowing from experience that Lily needed to process the renewed grief.

Once they deposited their bags in their room, Anastasia glanced over at Lily, who flopped on the bed numbly. "Still up for seeing the northern lights tonight?"

Lily shrugged and didn't meet her mother's gaze. "I don't know…"

Did seeing the memorial cross change her mind? I know I didn't want to come, but I don't want her birthday trip to be ruined. I need to salvage this... She tilted her head. "Didn't you say the University of Alaska-Fairbanks forecasts a good chance of seeing them tonight?"

"Yes. The K_p index is supposed to be a seven."

"So why not go out tonight?" She sat next to Lily, running hands through her daughter's hair. "That's practically guaranteeing seeing something."

A bit of silence stretched out before Lily sat up and leaned into her mother's side, prompting Anastasia to put an arm around her. "I just...I wish Dad was here. It feels wrong to do it without him. He promised to take me, after all." Her eyes glistened with the beginnings of fresh tears. "I thought that retracing the steps he should've taken would bring closure—make me feel closer to him, but all it's done is remind me of how much I miss him."

"I know, honey," she murmured, eyes misting while drawing Lily closer. "I know. I wish he was here, too." She kissed her daughter's head before a thought appeared in her mind like the sudden appearance of an auroral ribbon in the sky. "*But*...I bet he'll still be here with us in spirit..."

Lily, sniffling, blinked up at Anastasia. "You sure?"

Anastasia gave her a small smile. "Yes. I mean, you said he'd want us to have fun following in his footsteps, and we *did* manage to make it here. We have to do what he wasn't able to. We can't waste a clear, high K_p index night."

"What if doing this without him feels like too much?"

She nosed her daughter's hair. "How about we go somewhere close—the front desk gal recommended Ester Dome—and give it an hour? If you're overwhelmed after an hour, we'll come back."

Lily considered this then wiped up her tears with her sleeve. "Alright," she conceded with a hint of a smile to match her mother's. "Let's do it."

The twenty minute drive to Ester Dome passed in a flash. Anastasia parked the car and smiled, nudging Lily as she surveyed the horizon. They had the mountaintop to themselves.

"This looks like the perfect place. Let's get the camera set up and camp out."

Lily nodded, and the two women prepared for their chilly, hour-long vigil. However, the minutes dragged on, and there wasn't even a hint of those magical lights both had dreamed to see for over a decade.

I hope we didn't bring up the past grief for nothing, Anastasia fretted, examining her gloves. *I had a feeling this might be a bad idea. First, I put Lily through seeing the place where her dad died, and now she's being disappointed by the skies.* She bit her lip, leaning against the SUV. *She doesn't deserve this. The gas station visit already hurt her enough this evening...*

"I'm sorry to drag you out here," came Lily's voice to her left. Anastasia saw her slink closer for warmth, back from some pacing she'd done. She avoided Anastasia's gaze. "I thought it'd help...to see the lights...to do what Dad never could..."

"It's okay, sweetheart," Anastasia reassured her. "You have your dad's adventurous spirit...and persistence. You were bound to come here at some point." She kissed Lily's head.

"But I shouldn't have pressured you when you were scared of returning," Lily continued, not pacified in the slightest. Her eyes finally managed to hold her mother's, guilt dancing in them. "I...I understand how you feel...how much Dad's death hurt you..."

The older woman shook her head. "It's alright. We promised to take you at some point, and if anything, your dad would've wanted me to keep that promise for him." She slid an arm around Lily's shoulders. "Besides, we're here *finally*, so we should make the most of it."

"Are you sure?" Lily dishearteningly gestured at the sky. "It was supposed to be a good show tonight. The skies are clear, yet we haven't seen *anything*."

"I know," she sighed. "It all technically is a probability, even if the K_p index is high. You never know when or where the aurora will strike, even in the best places. That's why you're supposed to be patient." She pulled Lily closer. "Want to go back to the hotel and try again another night?"

"How long has it been?"

Anastasia glanced at her watch. "Fifty minutes." She raised an eyebrow at Lily. "Want to leave early?"

A silence crystallized in the frigid air before Lily shook her head. "No. I promised an hour. I'll keep my promise. Then, we can leave."

"Alright, sweetheart." She smiled. "And when we get back, we can get some cocoa."

A smile slipped out of Lily as she pushed off the car to pace again. "Sounds good, Mom."

Anastasia was about to lean back when a brightening gray splotch appeared against the star-strewn sky. *Could it finally be...?* She gestured at the splotch as it grew brighter. "Lily, look!"

Lily glanced there and squinted. "Is that really...?"

As if in answer, the gray gently unfurled into ribbons of greens, reds, and blues. The luminous ribbons undulated like dancing streamers until the glow illuminated the entire sky.

The two women ran to each other and embraced, shouting in joy and wonder as they watched the lights dance across the sky.

"Mom, did you hear that?" Lily's voice broke the silence as she separated from her mother and pointed towards the horizon. A green streamer of light separated from the main swirl of colors and descended towards the ground

"What do you mean? I don't hear anything."

Lily's eyes widened with surprise as they fixed on the streamer of light. "Dad?" She immediately sprinted towards the streamer of light, and it flowed over to meet her. "Dad!" When they met, the streamer flowed around her as if it were burying her in a warm hug. "You're here!"

Anastasia stared at the scene before her. *What in the world is going on...?*

"Mom, you've got to come here!" Lily's voice penetrated through her thoughts.

She blinked and saw a tendril of light reaching out towards her as if it were a hand beckoning her to join the luminous embrace it had engulfed Lily in.

"I can't forget my promise to you either," came a familiar male voice.

That's not *possible...* Anastasia froze. *But wait. That's* John's *voice. It is* him! *He didn't forget!* she realized. *Well, eleven years isn't 'no time', but better late than never.*

She needed no further invitation to dart over to join her daughter and the lights. When she reached them, the streamer flowed around her as well, the light somehow as comforting as if it were his physical body hugging her. As her vision began to blur, she murmured, "I missed you so much, John..."

"I miss you, too," Lily agreed, tears staining her face but eyes shining bright. "I wish you didn't have to leave."

The lights brightened around them, and Anastasia felt a gentle squeeze, almost as if it were a final hug before parting. She smiled. "He might be gone *physically*, but he'll always be in our hearts," she realized.

"Enjoy the light show," John's voice said. The edge of the streamer lightly touched Lily on the head then Anastasia on the cheek. Then, it unwound itself from the two women, the streamer swirling back up into the dancing colors of the sky as they looked on.

Story 6

Before, After, During

Augustin Cavalier

Whenever Josh tells this story, he usually begins with three sentences conveying relative senses of time. First: *It was before Thanksgiving, but after all the leaves had fallen*—evoking images of gray woods, not yet chilled by wintry winds or blanketed with fallen snow, and the strange period after Halloween which is occupied more and more by Christmas each year. Second: *This was after Troy Quartz drunkenly smashed his BMW into the big light-up sign by the road leaving a football game and got chewed out by his dad within earshot of half the school*—one of the most significant events for any adolescent around Melvinsburg in those years. Much was never the same after that, least of all Troy (socially, not physically), the sign (both socially and physically), and football games (more socially than physically).

But this story isn't much about Troy, but rather about Josh. Hence his third sentence: *This was during our senior year, when Andrew's father was dying, and I was still learning how to not be a huge jerk.* That last bit was true enough, but by the time Josh started telling this story, he'd gained enough humility that he probably over-emphasized his jerk-ness, if you ask me. But as it happens, I'm not Josh, and I don't tell this story the same way he does.

The Monday after the sign incident found the whole school discussing little else. *Did you know Troy's dad's class donated that sign? Huh, d'you think he did it on purpose then? That's it for our chances at the championship. How'd he even sneak alcohol from the bench?* You know, standard stuff, and practically none of it done out of any concern for Troy. He'd been at the top of the pecking order for two years, but between his earlier benching and now expulsion from the team, the school was about done putting up with him.

By lunch, I was about done with the whole subject. "I've been done with it since I got off the bus this morning, and Kay never cared in the first place," said Anna, my girlfriend at the time, as she and her friend Kayla took seats. "Ready to go visit Andrew's dad this weekend?"

"What's this about my dad?" said Andrew curiously, coming up with Josh close behind.

"*Eep!*" squeaked Anna, before trying to change the subject. "Andrew—it's Monday. Why aren't you and Josh sitting with the debate team?"

"Because they're all talking about Troy and the sign, and we guessed you wouldn't be," said Andrew, settling in. "Pass the salt, please, Zach."

"Good guess," I said, passing the salt. "So—about that project for Mr. Hayden, then—"

"No, wait. What's this about my dad and this weekend?" Andrew asked.

I looked over at Anna, who looked back at me, and finally at Andrew. "We, uh, we've been talking about going to visit him. The three of us, plus Josh, so four of us. Well, you'll be there too, so it'd really be five, which is probably the most that'll fit in the room—that is, if you don't object. We don't want to impose, but we would like to visit," Anna explained, awkwardly.

Andrew looked shocked for a moment. "I mean—I guess you

can," he said. "I wasn't exaggerating when I said he wasn't doing well; he'll probably be asleep the whole time, and even if he's awake he's barely able to talk. You really don't have to come, it's not—he's not a pleasant sight."

"Bro, we want to come anyway," I said. "And we'll try and make it like old times on the bus as much as we can."

"I'll bring our history textbook and the next study guide, then," said Josh. "And I know there's already Bibles there."

"I'll bring cookies and my crochet bag," said Anna.

Kayla waved a weatherbeaten copy of one of Lang's *Fairy Books*.

"I, uh," I started, but Josh had taken my original idea. "Oh—I'll come prepared to climb out the window!"

"You will not!" Anna proclaimed reflexively, but then she hesitated. "Well, if it's low to the ground, and it won't damage anything, and since this might be the last time we see him—then maybe just this once."

"Why would this be the last time we see him?" asked Josh.

Anna seemed caught off-guard. "Uh, I guess we might find time to go back? But our schedules and visitor hours conflict for the next while..."

Josh looked like he wanted to say more, but Andrew spoke up before he could. "Thanks guys," he said, sounding touched. "You—it means so much. Nobody else has even asked."

Kayla opened her mouth to reply, but at that moment, Billy May stalked over. "So, how about Troy, huh?" he interjected. "Serves him right, yeah?"

"Look man, we're not talking about that here. Go gossip with somebody else," I said.

"Nobody asked you, Zach," Billy shot back, before turning to stare at Josh. "Seriously, nothing? Not going to gloat about his misfortune? Maybe preach about how his 'immorality' has caused 'comeuppance' and 'punishment from God,' or whatever?"

"No," said Josh, staring right back. "I'm not, thanks."

"Hayden really got to you, huh?" said Billy. "Whatever. You're no fun anymore. Worthless dope," he concluded, drifting away.

"What's his problem?" asked Anna.

"Psychopathy," Kayla deadpanned.

We all cracked up. "Kayla!" said Anna. "You can't just say things like that!"

Whatever his motivations, Billy's attempts at provocation hadn't come from nowhere. You see, at the end of sophomore year, a Baptist revival meet had come through town (we'd previously thought them a thing for the history books), and Josh, then a star athlete and 'partier' along with Troy, had fallen in with them—and subsequently proclaimed to our whole lunch hour that he'd been "born again" and would never again touch alcohol or engage in "pre-marital relations." We'd all rolled our eyes and thought he wasn't fooling anybody, but to our astonishment he actually stuck to it—so obnoxiously, though, that he had a severe falling-out with Troy which resulted in his dismissal from the football team.

The long aftermath of that fiasco was the height of Josh's jerkness. Not only was he obnoxious towards his old friends, he also stopped ignoring people outside the 'popular crowd' and was positively insufferable to anyone and everyone who wasn't a dyed-in-the-wool Baptist. (I'd have a hard time believing anyone's ever used the words *papist* and *idolater* more than Josh did during that period.) Some of it was more funny than insulting, but the rest motivated us to try and prove him wrong, often finding our own wavering beliefs strengthened in the process.

Then, one weekend, Anna spotted Josh and Mr. Hayden in an angry shouting match in the supermarket parking lot. She couldn't really make out what they were saying, but after that, Josh abruptly went from spewing fire-and-brimstone on a daily basis to practically never, and somewhat awkwardly offered his hand in truce to all those he'd confronted directly. For a small few of us, the truce slowly developed into a friendship, one where Josh would smirk at jokes made at Billy May's expense right along with the rest of us.

"He's probably going to try again later," Andrew pointed out.

I groaned, putting my head in my hands. "This week's gonna be long, and I'm exhausted already. I just want it to be over, man."

"You sound like you want the year to be over, not just this week," said Andrew, raising an eyebrow.

"I kinda do, yeah," I said, peeking out at the others. "Josh, how about you?"

"I'll be content with getting through next period," he said gruffly, looking down and picking at his food. "Not really that hungry. See you later."

We watched him go, a bit shocked.

"What was that about?" I asked, lowering my hands.

"I think it was what I said," said Andrew, seriously. "He's—Troy was once his friend, remember, and, uh—he's not loud and brash like last year, but he's still the same person. If you get what I'm saying."

I blinked a few times. "You mean that he, what? Still thinks all those things he used to say, but doesn't say them?"

"If Billy or whomever keeps trying—" Andrew paused. "Look, Josh hasn't really talked to me about this, I'm kinda guessing and reading between the lines here. I don't know how much I should say."

"I thought he'd changed," I said. "After Mr. Hayden argued with him."

"People don't change overnight," said Kayla.

"But he did," I said. "Didn't he?"

Anna looked at me and tilted her head. "He was convinced overnight, maybe. But anger doesn't go away overnight."

"And he was angry before, too," said Kayla.

"Point," said Andrew, and sighed. "We should probably keep an eye out for him."

That was Andrew for you: his dad was on his deathbed, and he was still looking out for his friends.

I didn't share next period with Josh, but while everyone else was nodding off as our science teacher droned on, I thought about what Andrew had hinted at. What was going through Josh's head? Was he really as angry as before, only he now kept a lid on it? If he might think it about Troy, did that mean he still thought all those things about 'papists,' too?

By the end of class, my thoughts hadn't died down but focused, so I looked for Josh in the hallway while heading to our shared last period. His class had been directly across from mine, so he wasn't hard to find.

"Hey," I said.

"Hey," he replied, tonelessly.

"I, er," I tried to remember how I'd thought to start. "Don't listen to whatever Billy and those others have to say. Even if they come at you all week. Maybe even let us scare them off, yeah?"

Josh grunted in an affirmative manner.

"Good," I said. "This'll all blow over, and things'll go back to normal before we know it."

"Maybe they shouldn't," Josh grumbled.

"Huh?"

"Maybe they shouldn't go back to normal," he repeated, slightly louder. "Normal would be the debaucherous lifestyle of the popular crowd continuing as before."

"Uh," I said, a bit taken aback. "I mean, I don't like the 'debaucherous lifestyle' either, but this is high school, man. It's been like this forever. One random incident isn't going to change that, it's just going to make the school breathe down our necks more."

"I know that," Josh bit out. "I know that. But people have been scared straight over less. So long as there's a crack, the Lord can pry the door open wide."

"People...? Wait, is this about Troy after all?" I said, surprised. "Are you hoping he'll, what, have a 'come to Jesus' moment like you did because of this?"

"Not just him," said Josh. "The more people think about the whole situation, the more some will recognize that it could've been them. Or they might remember that sin is often punished by the Lord with misfortune."

"Wait," I said, stopping dead in the hallway. "You actually still think that? So you think what's happened to Troy is because God is angry with him or something?"

Josh turned back to look at me. "Why *wouldn't* God be angry with him?" he asked. "Look at how he's behaved since middle school. He's broken more than half of the Ten Commandments. Maybe even two-thirds. And it didn't 'happen to' him, he brought it upon himself."

"So was Billy right? You think God smited Troy, and you're happy about it?"

"He's alive and not even maimed—he's hardly *smited*," Josh fired back. "And I want him to repent and be Saved. If this is part of how the Lord causes that, then yes, I'm happy about it."

"I dunno man, that just seems kind of—wrong," I said, somewhat thrown. "Even if another's misfortune might lead them to God, it feels wrong to be happy about it. But that doesn't explain why you left lunch so abruptly."

"Because I didn't think about how I'll have to deal with extra goading until Andrew pointed it out," Josh retorted. "To hear people mock God, wanting me to take the bait so they can feel all righteous about it—why aren't you mad about that, too? These people think they're in absolutely no danger of going to Hell, they think Jesus is a big joke, and probably nothing I could say would make them take Him seriously."

"Maybe," I allowed. "But that doesn't mean we can't do anything. Are you praying for them, at least?"

"Yeah," said Josh, as if it was obvious.

"Well, that's good, I guess," I said, resuming the walk. "Being happy about misfortune still doesn't feel right to me, though. But we'd better get to class."

Josh opened his mouth for a moment, but then closed it again and said nothing the rest of the way.

We arrived in the classroom with little time to spare. I took my seat next to Anna, and Josh behind Andrew. Anna's brows furrowed as she looked at me, but I waved her concern off. *"Later,"* I mouthed.

Last period was honors literature with none other than Mr. Hayden. Under normal circumstances, it would've been nearly impossible to zone out for any more than a few minutes in his class, but today was an exception. The class was as intense and fascinating as ever, but my mind was elsewhere, trying to determine if I should let Josh be, or whether there was still something to be dealt with.

With some reluctance, I admitted to myself that happy feelings about Troy's misfortune weren't worth addressing further, seeing as most of us had at least a bit of schadenfreude about it. That left the frustration with the "pagans and apostates," as Josh sometimes called them: if that continued building all week, the result wouldn't be good. But how could he deal with it better? All the ways that came to my mind were things he'd previously mocked as 'papist superstition.' He'd likely be more tactful now, but I didn't think his rejection of them had changed.

My thoughts stalled. Then, at the front of the room, Mr. Hayden gestured widely as he made some point—and I realized that the solution was right in front of me: whatever had been said in their infamous argument, Mr. Hayden had clearly, despite his status as a known 'papist,' gotten through to Josh. Perhaps he would be able to do so once again.

After the bell rang and class was dismissed, I raised a hand as I packed up my notes.

"Yes, Mr. Jacobs?"

"This is kinda off-topic, Mr. Hayden," I said. "But if there were people who mocked God to your face, but you couldn't make them stop or convince them they're wrong, what would you do? Besides pray for them, I mean."

Josh shot me a look, and Mr. Hayden raised both eyebrows. "I don't think the administration would be very happy with me if I talked religion while on the clock, Mr. Jacobs."

"Oh," I said, deflated. "Not even hypothetically?"

"Not even hypothetically. But," and that mischievous glint of his appeared in his eyes, "perhaps *literature-ally.*"

"And what's that mean?" I asked.

Mr. Hayden steepled his fingers. "Do you know what we're going to read next spring?"

I didn't recall, but Anna did. "*The Canterbury Tales?*"

"Indeed. Now, do any of you know what the *Tales'* frame story is?"

"Uh," I said, trying to think back to when my older sister had talked about it at family dinners. "A bunch of people going to Canterbury?"

"And why, pray tell, were they going to Canterbury?" asked Mr. Hayden, leaning back. "Was it for the funs and the giggles? Or did they have some reason?"

"It was a pilgrimage, I think?" I said.

"Yes, but what's that, and why'd they do it?" Mr. Hayden asked, then answered his own question, "Because they had something to beg God for, or perhaps thank Him for, and regular old prayers just didn't seem enough. So they made a journey, not for the sake of their own amusements, but for God's sake, setting aside time and effort to grow closer to Him."

"But journeys were a lot harder then," said Andrew. "It wouldn't really be nearly as big a deal to get in a car and drive to some faraway place now."

"It isn't about the distance or the difficulty, exactly," said Mr. Hayden. "In medieval England, people would make pilgrimages to many more places than Canterbury, some of them quite close to their homes. All they needed was an intention, and a destination that was holy or set aside for God in some way."

"But it's not just the medieval English who made pilgrimages," I said. "Literature-ally speaking, I mean."

Mr. Hayden smiled. "Oh, no, of course not. The *Canterbury Tales* are simply the most famous example of a sort of literature that's likely been around as long as Christianity. There's surviving 'pilgrimage diaries' from many different times and places, from antiquity right down to the present day."

We pondered that for a few moments. "Thanks, Mr. Hayden," I finally said. "That helps."

"I suppose it'd be too much to hope that you'll crack open the *Tales* before next spring," he said with a half-smile. "But if any of you come to class already having gone on some sort of pilgrimage your-selves, that'll make discussions more interesting!"

We thanked him and departed. The rest of the afternoon passed in a whirlwind of routine, but that evening at parish youth group, I caught up with Anna and relayed the conversation I'd had with Josh in the hallway.

She was quiet for a few moments, before sighing. "I'm not that surprised, really," she said. "But how much does it matter?"

"I don't know," I said. "If he's just going to be on edge for the week, that's one thing. But I've been wondering if there's something else here. Troy's accident was entirely his fault, but d'you think—does Josh think that bad things don't *really* happen to good people?"

"What? Like—the 'prosperity gospel'?" she asked. "There's no way. He'd have to think Andrew's dad was secretly a monster or something rather than a committed Baptist for him to be dying of cancer, and Josh just doesn't think that. I can't see it."

"I don't know," I said again. "Maybe you're right. It was kind of a half-baked thought anyway."

The rest of the week flew by. Josh kept his cool, the drama simmered down like it usually did, and soon enough it was the week-end. I awoke Saturday morning to an unseasonably severe downpour, the rain coming down in sheets across the lawn outside. I was initially worried it might prevent me from visiting Andrew's dad with the others, as my mom wouldn't let me drive in such weather and my dad was away that week, but thankfully Anna and her father agreed to drive out of their way to pick me up.

Anna's dad dropped us off at the doors to the hospice. We signed in and headed up to Mr. Davis' room, finding Josh and Kayla already there, but no sign of Andrew. We took our seats, and I got a good look at Mr. Davis.

To tell the truth, he looked terrible. He was gaunt, looking like he'd aged decades in the months since I'd last seen him, his face shrunken and lacking its old roundness, the laugh lines turned into rows of wrinkles. He'd once looked more than a bit like Louis Armstrong, and maybe sounded a little like him, too, but that resemblance was gone. He'd never again get the chance to be the jolly man driving our bus, or to treat us like his sons and daughters (though he reserved the embarrassing endearments for Andrew), or to ask what we'd learned in history class each day—but above all, Andrew would be left parentless for the rest of his life.

We all just sat there, wondering if or when Andrew was going to arrive, not wanting to start anything without him. The minutes dragged on; after a half-hour, he finally appeared in the doorway, panting slightly, with the cuffs of his pants drenched and spotted with mud and his shoes looking like they'd been hastily wiped down, but otherwise dry.

"Hey man," I said, standing to greet him. "You okay? What happened?"

"What?" he asked, then glanced at his shoes and cuffs. "Oh. No, I'm fine. The storm knocked a tree onto my car overnight, so I walked here."

"Oh, Andrew, you should've called," said Anna. "We could've picked you up. Or Josh, probably, he's closer to you."

"No, no, it's fine," he said, not sounding angry or even upset. "I wasn't really planning to use it today anyway. I wanted to make a pilgrimage to that little glade on the top of Meadows Drive where there's the three big crosses standing, and I did. It was really nice."

"In this weather?" I said, astonished.

"I'd told the Lord a few days ago that I was going to do it, and He sent the rain anyway, didn't He? It worked out fine; I wore a poncho, I'm barely even wet."

"We're sorry about your car, though," said Anna. "Can we do anything to help?"

"No, no, seriously guys, it's fine," he said, sounding like he really meant it. "I'll call the insurance later. It'll all work out, I'm sure of it. Let's just enjoy this time together right now, okay?"

"Why'd—what'd you make a pilgrimage for?" asked Josh.

"To thank the good Lord for all the blessings He's put in my life. All of you, not least of all," he said, soberly; it wouldn't be until much later that I would consider what thoughts and feelings he must've had but wasn't letting on. "And it was worth it. Reaching the crosses at the top of the hill, I felt so spiritually refreshed."

Josh opened his mouth once, then twice. "Why'd—" he started. "What—" but in the end, he just put his head into his hands, skirted around all of us, and left the room.

This, rather than anything else, made Andrew sigh and look exhausted. "Just let him go," he said, as he took a seat. "He'll probably come back."

Anna opened up her crochet bag, and slowly we all started telling the unconscious Mr. Davis about school. I kept glancing at the clock; a half-hour went by without sign of Josh. His uncharacteristic behavior concerned me enough that I figured we shouldn't leave him alone indefinitely. "I'm going to go look for Josh," I announced, and walked out before anyone could protest.

I found him a few minutes later, staring out a window in a lounge at the end of the hall, hunched over and with his hands shoved into his pockets. I came up alongside him slowly and just stood there, looking out the window in silence.

"*It's not about you,*" he finally said.

"What?" I asked, confused.

"That's what Mr. Hayden said to me, in that argument in the parking lot everyone's so curious about. *Get over yourself, it's not about you.*"

"That's…kind of cliche, isn't it?"

"But he was right," Josh said. "I was arguing that somebody

needed to preach the Gospel to these people, he was arguing that I was doing a terrible job of it, I argued back that the Lord is almighty and can save them even if I wasn't witnessing well, and he retorted that *maybe God saves them in spite of you, did you ever think of that? And for whatever reason, I hadn't thought about it that way before.*"

"Okay," I said slowly. "But why's that on your mind now?"

"Because it's not about me again. Andrew's dad's dying, and I'm the one who's upset. He's at peace with it and even talking about blessings, while all I could think for weeks was that maybe Mr. Davis was going to get better, that the Lord would reward their faith, that death would be deferred, or something. But then I walked into that room for the first time in months, and saw Mr. Davis looking like that; and then Andrew comes in and he's still at peace, and I'm still upset about it. Maybe even angry about it. And he's just —not."

I couldn't think of anything to say to that, so I didn't. We stood in silence for a bit, until someone knocked on the open door. "Storm-watching party in here?" a voice asked, almost painfully earnestly.

I knew that voice: it was Fr. Nickels, our parish priest. He was very nice, but he had an unfortunate tendency to treat everyone below middle age with the absolute softest of kid gloves, though I'd never seen him do it in a hospice before. "Hello Father," I said, unenthusiastically.

"Oh, it's you, Zach! And who's this? Hello, I'm Fr. Nickels," he said, extending a hand. "Used to be Fr. Dollars, but I spent them all; tomorrow it'll be Fr. Dimes—you know how inflation is."

"Yes, I do," Josh ground out, not turning around. "Can you just leave us be?"

"Well, I don't want to intrude," said Father, his voice still far too warm. "But whenever people gaze out at a storm in silence, it often means there's something on their minds, and I just wanted to check in case you wanted to talk about it."

"No thanks, Father," I replied.

But Josh had other ideas. "Yes, I want to talk about death," he said, rounding on Father. "And why the Lord lets tragedies happen to good and faithful Christians. Anything to say about that?"

"Well, ah," Father stuttered, glancing around nervously. "I don't —the Book of Job, maybe?"

"I've read it," said Josh.

"Well," began Father, more serious this time—and then his face scrunched up in an odd way. "Once, when I was in seminary, there was this paper I had to read—I don't know why I'm remembering it now—something about the 'relative temporality of experience,' about how people get trapped thinking about the 'before's and the 'after's and really they should think more about the 'during's, because— something about God's grace and 'hope-unlooked-for.' It was very fascinating, but I'm not sure I understood any of it. Does that help?"

I didn't think that confused jumble of words was likely to help anyone, but at that point I just wanted Father to leave us in peace. "It's something to think about," I said, trying to sound agreeable. "Thanks, Father."

"You're welcome, Zach," he said, bright and cheerful once more, but looking like he wanted to disappear before Josh snapped at him again. "I'll leave you boys to it, then. Toodle-oo!"

I turned to Josh as Fr. Nickels left, hoping I wouldn't be greeted with a half-dozen new prejudices against my religion from that encounter. But to my surprise, he was just staring at the doorway with a dumbfounded look on his face.

"Uh," I started. "Josh?"

"Before, after, or during," he said, sounding dazed, like it was some kind of revelation. "I can't believe it."

"What?" I said. "You mean—that wasn't just a bunch of nonsense?"

"All this time," Josh said, ignoring my question, "I was thinking about all this as 'before' and 'after.' Before we graduate, before we enter the real world, before—before Andrew's father dies. Or after I found God, after I was baptized, after Mr. Hayden yelled some sense into me, after I gained all of your friendships," he explained. "But the

Lord says to ask for 'daily bread', and to 'take no thought for the morrow.' Job still trusts and praises the Lord, even in the midst of the —well, the *during*. And Andrew's been living that, while I couldn't even see it."

"Oh," I breathed. "Did—huh. I think I need some time to process that."

"So do I," said Josh, turning to look at me, and I could see something new in his eyes that I would recognize later as *hope*. "And I know we'll argue it to death after we do. But I think we're supposed to start by doing, and think about it later. And the doing right now is to go back to Mr. Davis' room, and be there for this particular 'during,' while he's dying, but he's not dead, not yet."

And, I tell you, we indeed did all those things. Not all on that day, of course, or even that same month. Before the year was over, Mr. Davis had passed on, and Andrew had moved in with Josh and his mother, and Josh had begun asking Mr. Hayden theology questions 'literature-ally' more than the rest of us combined.

But all that came after. In the moment, we were content with the *during*.

Story 7

Impressions

Catherine Broussard

Vibrations coursed through the frame of the building as the storm outside did its best to tear down this latest refuge, crafted for artistry by the artist herself. Hail clunked on the domed metal roof. Larger pieces left dents that would become more cracks if the roof took many more hits. She had called forth bowls from the ground with a simple song to catch drips of water from existing cracks. The leaks added a plunk and a plink to the medley within. A canvas, balanced on an easel too small for it, took up the majority of the main chamber. The work on it? Unfinished. Smatterings of color and dashes of detail in the corners, but the center left blank, for its artist was no longer at her place. Instead, she stood in the front chamber, pulling back the metallic curtain to watch the torrential downpour assail her shelter. Here, she could pretend the tears on her face were just the rain. Here, she could sink to her knees and cry out and have the thunder be heard instead. Here, she could curse the storm and love the torrents all at once.

You mustn't cry when I am gone.

But she must. She must shed tears now, because he was not yet gone, not truly, just not *found* yet again. Years had passed by since she stood on the cliffside and witnessed the world at war with itself, where the mountain range broke into pieces and a new sea was formed before her eyes, and her father in the midst of it all became *lost*, not destroyed.

She refused to believe what she saw with her own eyes when the sea swallowed the mountaintop and her father in one.

She refused to believe what she'd heard on the wind for the days she stood there, keeping vigil.

She refused to believe because her heart told her there was still a chance, however small.

She was stubborn like that. Her nose wrinkled, and she sniffed back tears that tried to keep falling. He'd told her her stubbornness would keep her alive. Against her chest, the cold metal of her father's pendant stung—never warm, never soothing, only cold and harsh on her skin like the rain that assaulted her face in this doorway. His last gift to her, before she was meant to be whisked away to safety that she'd refused. Safety that she had rejected, instead, chosen to stand and offer her voice to her father's battle. He hadn't been alone. He hadn't been without someone to fight for him. Fight she had, and fight she would, then *and* now. Back then, she had fought for the world. Now? She fought for him.

A flick of her hand shut the curtain with a shrill squeak of metal. She licked the salty tears from around her lips and strutted back towards the canvas she'd left. Her steps switched from clinks to clunks as she left the tiled entry and returned to the studio. She'd come so far, miles walked, days spent, and nights of effort wasted on something that didn't want to be and yet she would force it to be. The journey could've been over weeks ago, but she wasn't ready. Not yet. Not to face what was to come, not so unprepared. Drops of water hit her head, cooling the heat that had risen with the release of her cries. One day, maybe, she would learn how to call waterproof shelters to rise from the grasses and metals hidden in the ground—but she'd yet to harness that power. A little fall of rain could hardly hurt her when her heart had been torn and stitched together again and again by time itself.

Blank spaces that remained on the canvas mocked her while she walked about it, looking at her pots of pigments and cups of brushes. The battle wasn't over. Couldn't be over. She'd prove it, and then *even the others* would have to believe her. By the time she finished both painting and journey, they'd understand. Then they'd have to join her fight to find him again. To keep him from the clutches of the one who still prowled the world, hidden somewhere like a snake coiled in its den. To restore all that had been lost. To reunite her with her father, that was all she wanted, and she was close. The journey would be through when she crested the next hill—the painting far less close to completion than she wished it would be by now.

A soldier fights til battle is won.

Bringing a half-finished work would be worse than bringing nothing at all. She pinned her hair back again and took up a paint brush, tapping it on the side of the cup it'd rested in for far too long while she'd wrestled with her mind. It'd still function. It had to.

Starting again was like a rock picking up speed while it rolled on a grassy hill. She soon found herself lost in the work. By the time she put down her brush, wiping the smudges of paint from her fingers onto her tunic, the world was silent again. No rain. No storm. She begged the wall to give her a window. It obeyed, and out of the opening she looked.

The ground had more likeness to a lumpy ice field with a few scattered bits of grass poking up and around the hailstones than to a valley of green. Overhead, the clouds themselves became pierced with rays of sun, for the storm lost its hold, unsuccessful in its own mission. It would try again later. Always it returned. Always with a greater vengeance. She had to wonder if it was sent after her by the dark figure who haunted her memories, but for now, she had only her thoughts for company, *again.*

Before it would return she needed to ensure her shelter was ready. It took her the better part of an hour to repair the damage to her simple shelter as the roof took the brunt of the beatings this time. Once every dent was popped out and every threatening crack made no more, every woven swatch patched with new braids of grass, she stood in front of the canvas. Only its center remained blank now. She didn't usually paint like this. Her tutor would be appalled to see her process for this, but it was all she could do, the only way she could get the image from her mind at all. Was it progress if it still made her heart pound and her memories ache to think of what would have to come forth to finish it? She picked a brush up again, the cool smoothness of the paint that worked its way onto the handle a welcome relief to her hands. At least that remained a comfort.

The paints, despite being heavy and rich as they were, would begin to dry soon. She'd wasted days here and it showed. Even now, despite it all, nothing about the painting pleased her. Usually, she could find solace in the way a painting would come together, revealing itself bit by bit, stroke by stroke. It wasn't enough. She couldn't leave it like this. He'd be disappointed if she did. He'd tell her he wasn't *mad*, no, just that he expected something more of her. The brush in her hand trembled with the shaking of her fist until it snapped from her grip, and the pieces flew with the force of her displeasure. The splintered wood hit the canvas itself, bits landing in the still damp paint of the edges, and bouncing off of the untouched center.

Finish work once it's begun.

A growl echoed from her throat to the top of the domed roof. Nothing had torn the painting, but as she leaned forward, dropping the remnants, she could see she'd have to coax each piece out of the paint if she wanted to save this work. She didn't want to put off finishing it anymore. She had to finish it here. It was the only thing keeping her from where she wanted to be, because they needed to *see*, so she could speak. If she could speak, they could hear her and know her truth. Its unfinished state tormented her on travels so far, made her pause for months whilst her own craft betrayed her. She wouldn't wait any more.

Her heart longed to enter into the house over the hill, full of life and song and laughter. On the clearest of evenings, in the winter when the bitter cold made the sound travel its furthest, she could hear and yearn.

She'd come so far, so close to her goal. Soon she'd have the proof she needed. This would be a memory saved. Secured. Established in a way that would mean she could voice the memories that burned her mind and scourged her dreams, ones she couldn't give sound to because talking would make them real. She'd never been able to share about what she'd seen—no—but she could paint it. She could speak, then, about a painting. She could point at the parts and explain why what happened had happened. She could tell them of how her father faced the dark figure, begging him to remember their friendship, and how he was forced to fight instead. How they rose above the mountains themselves and became locked in a battle that ran for days, time she couldn't track even though she'd tried. How she'd seen him falling —and the mountains breaking around him, creating a new sea, while the triumphant one cackled and crowed, lightning and wind echoing him and taking him away in a storm of victory while her father sank. Sank, but his song did not fade in her eyes. They'd have to believe her.

The first splinter she pulled free with her fingers, leaving an impression of itself on the surface, and getting a burnt sienna orange on her nails. The impression gave a depth to the far off mountainside, like a chip was missing from it, better matching the scene in her mind. She narrowed her eyes and took out more splinters, each causing the same effect. The biggest one had smeared color when it landed, leaving an imprint of an unexpected light reflecting in the blue of the sea. A bit of red and blush and gold, scattered and smeared in a way that could be mistaken for something beautiful. A portrait of a childhood friend came to her mind's eye, with his red and blush and gold on his face. Sunchild, he'd been called once, his features reminding others of nature's glorious light. She'd, likewise, been called Daughter of Midnight—for her features recalled the night sky as much as his golden ones brought forth the sun. Sunchild and Daughter of Midnight. Friends. Perhaps they would've been more, if the world would've been kinder.

The memory turned sour. *He* wasn't the one she lost that fateful day. He became lost later. Not merely lost. *Taken.* Last she'd heard, last she'd been allowed to know, his location was unknown. Holding her breath for two was too much. Perhaps, though, if her father was found—he could help find Sunchild again. If there was a chance for one, why not a chance for both? They'd all spent many a day together, laughing, singing, rejoicing until the sky became painted in colors by clouds. Neither could be gone from this world yet—it would simply take time to uncover where they went—like uncovering the impression behind a splinter of wood and finding a memory.

Always give homage to the setting sun.

She tossed the last of the splinters onto the ground and stared at what she'd done. Until now she'd always been afraid of texture in her work. Smooth and safe strokes were her friends, easy to manage and more forgiving when her stroke went awry—just a thin layer to cover or scrape off. That worked best when she worked fast. The longer she waited to strike at her canvas again, the thicker her paints became resting out on her palette. She faced that consequence now and when she tried to pull that thin stroke across, it left a thick, stodgy line in its wake. Bumps and lumps, where it would dip and then dump far too much paint in one place.

This time she bit her cheek and turned her brush—a repaired one —around to nudge the lump of half-dried paint along, pressing a little too hard and instead denting the pigment where it rested. Another impression. The little round mark was like a bubble on the surface of the sea, frothing as it consumed the mountains around. She could see it rocking and crashing, heaving and hawing, in an unnatural way as if commanded by the discordant figure she hadn't dared to put onto the canvas yet.

She tried it again, pressing the tip of the handle of the brush into another area of half-dried paint. It worked. It worked too well. That which she tried to avoid, texture, would be the key to this painting. The palette in her hand, messy as her mind, reimagined itself. She dipped the tip of the brush's *handle* into the white, swirling it to get a thick glob that mixed with some of the icy blue she'd spent an hour perfecting the day before and pressed it onto the canvas. Dot by dot, she built up the frothing of the waves. Point by point, she captured their power and their wrath. Pressing by pressing, she finished the layer.

She stepped back, examining the progress. The scene in her mind came to life bit by bit, slowly revealing itself, and with each addition it revealed more of the memories of her world stopping. Her world had stopped twice already in her life. But those in the house over the hill—they didn't know *how* her world had stopped that second time. They only knew *what* had occurred. Because the dark figure, the one she refused to paint yet, had told the tale in his own way as he continued his course of carnage. He'd chosen to let her live, though that could change with his whim like the path of a storm.

Sometimes she wished he wouldn't have been so generous. She'd prayed she wouldn't have to endure—to endure would take a strength she had never wanted to find within herself. She'd wished she wasn't stubborn enough to continue in her journey to share what she knew. Many others would've given up. The thought brought a fresh wave of heat to her eyes and soreness to her throat—but that wound wasn't one she wanted to pick at today. That wound would heal with time. The one she painted would fester if she didn't air it out to the world.

She couldn't put the figure on the canvas yet. His visage haunted her and his laughter echoed in the depths of her mind. He seemed more a caricature of a man than one who belonged among mankind now.

With a clatter, the brush fell from her hand and to the floor. She blinked. In front of her was a canvas with less of an empty center—but its surroundings weren't yet through. She needed more than the end of a brush to build the layering she wanted for the mountains and the cliffs.

Let life continue when I am through.

She ran outside and picked up a melting piece of hail and grabbed a few blades of grass, varying sizes, to help build up the next layers on the painting. The hail—still large enough to fit in her palm—she pressed onto a thick swath of greys and browns and black and green that became textured like a mountainside. Rough like rocks. Sharp like stones. As the hailstone shrunk from the heat of her hand, so did the impressions it left, increasing its ability to aid her work. Water dripped from the ice, and with her persistent coaxing it could even cut its own rivulets and cracks into the rocky visage. Colors blended as she picked up and pressed the hail again and again. The combined techniques of painting, pressing, and even pleading by the melody she hummed slowly brought the memory to life on the canvas in a way she hadn't even thought possible. For the first time she could see before her what she'd only seen reflected within her mind for years, a scene frozen, a moment captured, reminding her of all that had been taken. Her father. A friend. A life she'd loved to live.

She clutched the hailstone tighter. The cold froze the fury within her. Methodical work occupied her thoughts, letting soft songs escape her lips and remind her of what she'd once had. Days of running through hillsides with Sunchild, nights of watching the stars with her father and mother at her sides, mornings of dancing in the dawn, times when the simplicity had bored her. She longed to be bored by the simple things again. Her hand went numb like the grief she'd hidden back in the depths of her heart, in the places that were dark in her mind. The welling of tears could come with the fire of indignation's cooling.

Reaching to the small woven table beside her, she grabbed a wide, flat blade of grass. The mountains and the scraggly and craggy rocks were done. She needed to add color and shade for the world that was made more alive and the songs that were sung at the hour of finality—like rays from the sun, like strokes of color from the heavens, like layered and textured light that brought both hope and despair with its presence. Capturing the essence of songs in art always challenged her, even though she could see the songs in the air herself if she wanted—if she so tried. The pendant under her clothes again flashed with its cold. Begging. Pleading. She'd refused to use it outside of necessity, for it belonged more to her father than her, but the times she had worn it—she'd seen what he could see. The world unmasked and alive in a way that intoxicated her, filling her with wonder and awe in ways that nothing else could. She craved it. She hated it. She loved it and loathed it. In her mind's eye she brought back the first scene she'd watched through its lens, the one on the canvas, and began building her pressed layers of pigments.

She pressed blades of grass into reds and rouges and purples and oranges, filling in that center spot where all would radiate into catastrophe. A halo of nothing holy but everything profane, the start of work on the discordant one who gave her reason to learn what hatred meant.

When she'd first found herself on the run from his continued influence in the world, she forsook painting for the sake of productive things. No reason to put the brush to the canvas when she had to find how to live on her own. Settled in a role, in a place, in a way that gave her direction—she'd found herself with the desire to share, no longer held back by fear. Years of not being understood—where no one would know what had happened if she didn't share it, and she couldn't speak it. Couldn't sing it. Her willingness to share wasn't able to counter the terror that she felt in her mind at contemplating telling the story.

Yet a few weeks ago, when she'd started her journey across the continent to find the ones who had once loved her like their own, she'd woven herself a canvas, a desperate attempt, and discovered she *could* paint it.

An artist can find inspiration new.

Hours passed by. Broken blades of grass littered the floor, and puddles of water formed a pool around her bare feet, forgotten by her as she stood lost in the miasma of artistry. Her shelter shook in the winds that whirled around anew. Since she started this journey not a day had gone by without the assault of multiple storms, the world's attempt to hold her back, to keep her from reaching where she needed to be. To keep her from sharing what she needed to share. She'd often given into the storms and let them pound away her thoughts and her desires to right the world's wrongs. In the rain and wind, it was easy to lay back and pretend to drown in their strength. Not anymore.

This time, she didn't stop to go cry in the door, to scream with the thunder. She mixed a color on the palette that would hide any other color, that would destroy any other shading and layering; it would be a void wherever it touched. That's how the discordant one was. Not a man, but a void, lacking all that was good in the world, all that was beautiful. His voice like a siren's call could bring people in, and it had lured her father until he broke free. Then the mountains broke with her father's attempts to sing humanity back into the other one, the discordant one of the void.

His form took shape. A pure shadow in the midst of the lights. To give him depth, she lit a piece from a broken paintbrush on fire and pushed the flame into the paint itself, extinguishing it and creating cracks and scorches that no coloring could imitate. Dark blues and yellows brought the needed color to his face, and white lines, used sparingly, showed his eyes. He had beautiful eyes. Green darker than emeralds in the ocean, dotted with gold that reminded her of Sunchild's, as it was proper for the child to bear the image of the father. Though the gold of the eyes of the discordant one had all but disappeared in this battle she'd witnessed, no longer like the other one she'd known.

She'd long avoided the discordant one. He terrified her mind, and her slumber would never be peaceful so long as she was alone in knowing the extent of his capabilities. The horrors he could unleash. Yet placing him on the canvas like the void he was made him seem...conquerable. The mountains may fall and hills become dust in his wake yet he was still, at the core of it all, *a man* though he'd forsaken mankind for dissonance. She stared at his form, hand shaking again, and he did not seem so monstrous as he would in the nightmares. A terror, one that still threatened to break the fragile good that remained, yet she could look at him and her knees did not shake.

But she'd been running even more from putting the one she loved into the image. He was the discordant one's foil; in all the dark, he was light. In all the chaos, he was order. In all the noise, he was a voice still, small, and constant. She looked down at her palette, its swirls of color all worked into one except along the edges by now, and it would not do. The violence of the rains outside that had begun again could not match the swelling of loss in her mind as she saw him sinking into the waves that churned and dashed with the mountainside atop—still a glint of his song she caught. Still a shimmer of what could be—and she knew.

His song would be golden. Like the last light she saw before he disappeared beneath the sea, like the sun as it rises in the morning, like the glint of the stars at the height of midnight, like the flames of a fire, like the trim on his cloak—like the rim of the pendant he'd given to her.

From storms of grey to skies of blue.

Seated on the ground in front of her canvas, she dug through the bag of colors she'd amassed in her years of travel and running. Some paints she'd purchased from merchants, some she'd made from flowers and others from finely ground minerals she'd pulled from the ground. Not this one. She'd created it, using some flakes of gold. Coaxing it into the medium. Mixing it with care, pleading with it to be akin to the paints she knew. She hadn't dared to try it out yet, holding onto it for the opportune time.

Thunder rattled her refuge again. Wind whipped through the window and threatened to drop the canvas on top of her. She asked the window to close, and it did. This would be the last storm she'd face before she found the solace she sought. Before she could bring with her the image of what she'd lived through, what she'd seen. Her father deserved to have his moments remembered in accuracy, that others might believe he could be found too.

At last she found her golden paint. It had rolled under one of the benches along the wall, and for this she returned to the brush—no need to press to create the ghost-like figure of her father, as he shimmered beneath the waters of the churning sea. The texture she'd layered, the grief she'd released into the piece, made him hard to see—and that was the point of it all. He was not lost. Merely hard to see. Waiting to be found again. She hummed the way he'd taught her, reaching low like to the ground and high as to the stars, warming up the voice that she'd made rough with screams and tears, and it soothed not only her tired throat but also her hand that would take these last strokes—his teaching guiding her hand even though they were far apart.

She took a brush with the tiniest tip, a hair or two wide, and traced his eyes. They stared at the admirer of the painting. A softness in their strokes. A glimmer like the glimmer of the gold.

Then it was done. She dropped her jaw to open her mouth, and her voice rose to an uproar that challenged the storm outside until she heard it no more. It would batter her mind, her will, her being no more. She stood in the door. The rain ceased, the sky filled with blue. Clouds ready to paint the sky itself with the fading colors of day.

With care, she packed all she had. Now she was ready to speak, to share, to show what she'd seen. It wouldn't just be her words—he'd be there too, on the painting and alive in her heart like she believed him to be in the world. The canvas she carried out last, after it dried and she could wrap it with care, to the valley where the sun shone and the grass was broken by hail and wind, so that she might finish her journey to the other side. For a moment, a brief and blessed moment, the wind tickled her ear with a voice that sounded like his.

Always remember that I love you.

Story 8

The Imperishable Stars

Paige Guerra

"Tell me what is yet to happen, for today has already happened and gone," the great king—may he live, prosper, and be well—requested a prophecy from the oracle. "What lies ahead?"

The high priest bowed deeply, considering his words before giving a careful reply. "The sleeper says 'I am awake.' The land is laid waste. Destruction is a fact. Ruin is reality. What was done will be undone, and Ra will begin his creation anew."[1]

"And what of myself?" asked the king, his dark brow creasing in curiosity. "If everything will perish, what is to become of me?"

Swallowing his uneasiness, the high priest spoke. "Ra distances himself from mankind, yet his rays remain visible now, as they were for the ancestors. The sand claims the desert before it, but the winds will reveal what once was lost."

* * *

---

1. From the *Prophecy of Neferty*, an ancient literary text from the middle kingdom Egypt (c. 2040-1782 BC)

Cairo was hot. Hotter than the devil's own armpit.

Despite having spent eighty-something years in the inescapable Florida heat, Geraldine had never felt the scorching sun quite as strong as this. She'd wandered that emotional desert of widows for years now, and yet neither could have prepared her for the positively oven-like quality of a Saharan summer.

Tattered awnings, long faded from deep reds to dusky pinks, stretched across the market, doing little to stave off the sun's unrelenting beams. A sensory deluge of warm spices, colorful fabrics, and tinkling glass lanterns were spread all down the street before her, trailing off into a distant blur. The marketplace was unlike anything she'd ever seen, and Geraldine felt inexplicably pulled toward each stand, mesmerized by every little trinket and bauble. She moved to dab away a bead of sweat that had all but evaporated before she could reach it.

Unsure of what she was searching for—maybe nothing in particular at all—she took her time, carefully inspecting the wares while vendors tried in broken English to convince her that their mass-produced curios were one of a kind. After an hour, nothing she found was *quite* the right souvenir for her long awaited trip to Egypt. Geraldine turned down another tight alleyway, this one sandwiched between two rough, sand-colored walls.

"What you seek is seeking you," said a deep voice. A man in a white *keffiyeh* sat behind a small table to her right, gesturing for her to come closer. The table was hardly the size of a TV tray, spread with a deep purple cloth, and occupied by one lone necklace. Geraldine stepped forward, drawn in by its simplicity more than by the merchant's vague comment.

"How do you know what I seek?" she asked flatly.

"Someone so wise and beautiful deserves an artifact of an equal measure," he cooed. Geraldine's face wrinkled further, narrowing her eyes at the man and the leather corded necklace. His use of the word *artifact* was not lost on her. Clearly, he wanted her to believe this was something special, something ancient.

"Ha." Geraldine jabbed her finger at the man. "Wrong. I seek to browse the market without being interrupted by your jabbering." She began to turn away, but a wave of curiosity stopped her.

The necklace's pendant was made from stone or white marble, carved into an oblong shape that was small enough to fit in the palm of her hand. Geraldine lifted it gently from the table, and a few granules of sand sprinkled the purple cloth where it had rested. A tingle of recognition surged through her. Upon closer inspection, the pendant was the unmistakable shape of an underscored oval.

"A cartouche," Geraldine observed. The stone in her hand felt lighter than she'd expected. She ran a thumb over the center of the oval, feeling the worn, carved shapes beneath the pad of her finger. "What does it say?"

"It is very old," said the vendor, ignoring her question.

Geraldine eyed him again. Old did not mean worthless—something young people everywhere constantly forgot. "And?"

"Difficult to make out," he said.

The carved hieroglyphs *looked* like all the others she'd seen adorning the various collectables scattered through the market. A twisted rope, a standing bird, a simple square, a stalk of reeds. It was difficult to tell, after centuries of wear, where the edges of the characters ended and the base of the pendant began. She didn't know any Egyptian, but there was one thing she knew for certain.

"It's a name," she said thoughtfully. Cartouches were always depicted as scrolls, the name or title of an ancient pharaoh or nobleman encircled within.

"Right you are, though we do not know whose," said the man. "All of the archaeologists I've brought it to have been unable to decipher it. Evidently, he was not a king worth knowing."

Something about the statement struck her. Here she was, four thousand something years in the future, holding on to the identity of a person in the palm of her hand. Holding on to a forgotten memory, clutching at long-faded shadows.

"Twenty pounds?" she asked. It was a fool's price if this was truly an artifact of the ancient world, but for some reason she couldn't name, the necklace was just the sort of souvenir she'd been hoping to find.

To her surprise, the merchant didn't haggle. He only shook her hand, nodding, and the pendant was hers.

A few hours later, seated on the barge that would bring her further up the deep sage waters of the Nile, she wondered what this Egyptian might have been like. How different would their lives have been? How similar? Had this been a once great king? A high priest? An honored laborer? Geraldine slipped the leather cord over her head and held the pendant out in front of her. Did he, too, long to be remembered, only to be slowly and methodically erased by the sands of the desert and the relentless passage of time?

Geraldine felt so old nowadays, and she had no one left to tell about this adventure—no family, no husband, few acquaintances, and even fewer whose names she bothered to know—but still, she had traversed land and sea and sky to fulfill this dream of seeing Egypt. All things considered, it was far more hot and miserable than she'd ever imagined. Still, she had come, despite the cost, and the mileage, and the naysayers—wretched old loons who wouldn't leave their apartments had it not been for the caretakers' persistent nagging. Her body was failing her. But her heart? Her heart was determined. Her mind was sharp. Her *spirit* was young, and that was what had convinced them to let her go.

She squinted out against the bright sun, watching wobbly reflections in the dark water glide beneath the hull of the long, thin boat. Three wide, piercing teeth of pyramids in the distance rose into the bluest sky she'd ever seen. The sight almost brought tears to her eyes, and she might have cried, were she not so dehydrated.

For decades, long since she'd decided to stop keeping track of the years, Geraldine had wanted to see these legendary ruins with her own eyes. In all her imaginings, she was not this wrinkly and bespectacled, nor alone, but she was here all the same: Saqqarah, the resting place of the god-kings.

As the ferry slowed to a halt against the soft silted sand, the guide let down from the canopy a long plank, nearly the length of the boat. It stretched across the water from a small gate at the front to the dry, packed sand several yards away.

Geraldine watched from behind thick glasses as the tourists ahead of her scurried onto land like rats, single file across the narrow gangway, chittering among themselves in various tongues. She waited until most of the people had cleared, and then slowly made her way out from beneath the shade of the canopy and into the blinding light.

The sand beneath her feet was blistering, and every molecule of dirt and dust that wormed its way into her shoes felt like a hot coal against her leathered skin. Eventually, the sands gave way to a foot-printed path that stretched out into the necropolis, where the rest of the tourists had gone.

Her foot caught against a half-buried stone, and she stumbled forward, almost scraping her knee against the ground. Grumbling to herself, she righted and continued along the path. There was no longer anyone around to help an old woman struggling to traverse the sand. She was alone, as usual.

When she finally crested the dune, what remained of her breath was stolen away. The monuments of Saqqarah rose against a vibrant blue sky. She couldn't tell if it was the heat waves, or if she was tearing up, but the whole scene looked fuzzy and warped, the blocky pyramid and pillars swaying in her vision.

Once she reached the gate, Geraldine paused again, stretching out a hand to feel the rough stone of the pillars, to be sure she wasn't dreaming. She was really here. Dust crumbled from the wall at her touch as her fingers traced the outline of millenia-old hieroglyphs.

It was beautiful. Not just the artistry among the carved and painted walls, not only the way the limestone stood, brilliant white against the sun-washed desert, but the very act of standing next to a structure so incomprehensibly older than she was made her feel... something. Young? No, her old bones felt every bit of age, every bump on the ground that threatened to trip her again. In fact, she needed somewhere to sit, catch her breath, and take it all in.

She found a suitable looking slab of limestone near the main pathway, checking for any remnants of hieroglyphics before leaning against it. A hot breath of wind blew across the site, scattering sand and debris into the air, and pressing the cartouche pendant against her chest. Geraldine held it in her hand as she watched the dust swirl.

Who were you? she wondered. *Are you buried somewhere out here in the sand? Did they forget you like they're going to forget me?*

A sharp prickling sensation pulled her from her thoughts. The wind was picking up, peppering her face with grains of sand, and she pushed her glasses higher on the bridge of her nose to keep the granules out of her eyes. White hair whipping across her face, Geraldine surveyed the area, which was now shrouded in a haze of dust that obscured the far side of the ruins.

A sandstorm.

Minutes ago, the sky had been clear. She strained to remember what the guide on the boat had said about an unexpected dust storm, a *habub*, he had called it. Would he have let them off the boat if they could be in danger? Geraldine looked around, unable to spot any tourists or site workers nearby to ask what she should do.

Pulling her head covering across her face to shield herself from the sand, she surveyed the area for a nearby spot that might better protect her from the wind. Across the path, a set of wide stone steps led down into darkness, flanked on either side by tall, intricately carved walls. The entrance to the step pyramid that towered at the center of the complex seemed as good a place as any to shelter from the ever-increasing assault of wind and sand, and she had planned to explore it anyway.

Carefully, she made her way toward the set of stairs, gritting sand between her teeth, each footfall becoming more uncertain as the storm continued to build. The wind threatened to topple her over. It became difficult to tell if she was making any progress, if she was still headed in the right direction, until she'd descended far enough for the walls to stave off the worst of the harsh gusts.

Only a few more steps, she thought, but each one was agonizingly slow as she strained to stay upright against the barrage. She wondered how the other tourists were faring, further out near the open desert, fully exposed to the storm. Fighting against the wind, Geraldine could not tell if anyone had made it into the pyramid entrance ahead of her. She stepped closer toward the doorway.

Once she crossed the threshold, the air around her stilled. Even though the sun outside had been scorching and bright, the cloud of sand had descended upon the necropolis and obscured all but a rusty haze of daylight that spilled into the entrance. She felt her way along the wall, hoping she wouldn't damage any of the ancient art on the delicate walls of the tomb. Outside, the wind howled and moaned as it tore through the site.

It was cooler beneath the surface, a welcome relief, though she could hardly see anything at all. The storm must have knocked out whatever power was needed to light the clinical fluorescents that would illuminate the walls. Just her luck. She'd come all this way, only to be stuck underground in the dark, without any light to see the remnants of this magnificent pyramid's intricate hieroglyphs.

Geraldine took about a dozen intrepid steps forward before her shoulder bumped into the form of a person standing in the darkness. "Oh, excuse me," she said, reaching her hands forward to steady them both. Her hands were met with a man's bare chest, and she withdrew them in surprise. "What are you doing?"

"Trying to find my way, as you are," said a man's low voice.

"Well I can't see a damned thing," Geraldine said. It occurred to her then that her phone might have a flashlight function, or at least the meager backlight of the screen could help them navigate their way in the dark. Geraldine fumbled around her bag, fishing for the device. When she found it, she flipped the cover open, casting a blueish-white glow that brightened their faces, but not much else.

The man in front of her was not particularly young or old—

younger than Geraldine, of course, everyone was nowadays—but older than the men who had helped sail the barge of tourists up the Nile from Cairo. His dark eyes were rimmed with kohl, complementing his tanned skin and short, black hair. She turned the screen toward him, illuminating him more fully, and saw he was dressed in a skirt of white linen. He looked as though he'd walked right out of the sarcophagus that once was buried here, like one of the paintings on the walls surrounding them had come to life.

"Where have you come from?" the man asked, looking back at her with curiosity.

Geraldine couldn't place his accent. "Outside," she replied, gesturing behind herself. She expected him to laugh, or scoff, but instead he nodded knowingly.

"The sandstorm."

She stepped forward and shone the light closer to his face, unable to recall reading anything in the tour pamphlets about there being live reenactments at the historic sites here. "Who are you?"

"You are wearing my pendant," he said matter-of-factly. "Who are *you*?"

She looked down at the stone artifact hanging around her neck, and the corner of her mouth ticked up in a smirk; she could play along. "I bought it at the market this morning. The man there said it was unable to be translated. If it's yours, what does it say?" she challenged.

"My name: Sekhemwyhotep."[2]

Geraldine froze and stared at him, having not expected an answer. A strange sense of familiarity washed over her. His name was *what?* It certainly sounded like an Egyptian pharaoh's name. But how could that be possible? She was starting to wonder if the desert sun had made her go completely insane.

---

2. Sec-EM-way-HO-tep, ancient Egyptian, meaning roughly "the two lands are at peace." The inverse name, Hotepsekhemwy, is the name of a real pharaoh from the second dynasty (c. 2890-2686 BC) whose name has been found among the hieroglyphs at Saqqarah, where Geraldine is visiting.

He smiled, sensing her confusion. "I have many names. A throne name, a Horus name, a given name. You can call me…Amal."

"Amal," Geraldine repeated, testing the name in her mouth. Something mysterious had happened, something very strange indeed. She hefted the carved stone in her hand. "Am I dead?"

The man gave a breathy laugh, but did not answer.

Geraldine tried to recall the circumstances which brought her to this dark tunnel in the midst of a stranger. When had she last seen another person? Not since the sandstorm started. Though she had made a point to keep a respectable distance from the rest of the tourists, she would have remembered seeing Amal before, if he had traveled here with them.

Geraldine released the amulet from her grasp and felt for her heartbeat. Her fingers pulsed with a steady lub-dub. She pinched the wrinkled skin that hung from her forearm and yelped. How strange. She still *felt* alive. If this was death, it was rather underwhelming. She tried not to dwell on the thought.

Amal stepped away from the soft glow of the screen, closer to the wall on their left. He peered into the dark, as if he were reading the hieroglyphs carved there with ease. "I thought I had completed the final task. It appears I have not."

"Task?" asked Geraldine. "What do you need to do?"

"Prove my worth," he said simply.

Don't we all, Geraldine thought to herself. Wasn't that why she had come all this way, to prove that she still could? "Any great ideas on how to do that?"

Amal pondered this, and then nodded. "Walk with me, I believe I know the way."

Geraldine hesitated for a brief moment before accepting the stranger's arm. She felt no sense of danger, only an overwhelming curiosity to hear what this man might say next.

Linking his arm through hers, Amal led her at a slow but steady pace through the dark hallways, expertly avoiding the walls and guiding her around corners she could hardly see. They walked without speaking for a few long moments while Geraldine tried and failed to sort out for herself what exactly was happening. Where was he taking her? Was this some mischievous worker playing a joke on her? Or was she somehow actually speaking to this "Sekhemwyhotep?"

Amal broke the silence first. "Names have power. I have given you mine, what is yours, that I may acknowledge it?"

It was a reasonable enough request. "Geraldine," she said. "My name is Geraldine."

"Greetings, Geraldine," Amal said slowly, deliberately, as if the words themselves held a kind of weight. "I am glad to have a companion on this journey."

"Where are we going?" she dared to ask.

Amal looked wistful. "To the imperishable stars."

Well, that didn't really answer anything. In fact, it only served to raise more questions, but she didn't want to insult Amal by asking what he meant. Instead, she held the phone out in front of her to try and light the way. Turn by turn, the dim light seemed to bring to life the carvings on the wall beside them, casting shadowy figures across the floor as they passed.

At the next intersection of hallways, Amal slowed, peering closer to read the hieroglyphs again.

"What does it say?" Geraldine asked, failing to recognize any pattern among the characters. She held her phone closer to the wall.

Amal pointed down a line of carvings. "This section here describes ways for the dead pharaoh to obtain the proper offerings to the gods, if the priests haven't brought any for him to use. It's crucial that I bring the right gifts to please them."

In the dark, Geraldine smiled as she realized his mistake. "So you *are* a king?"

"I am."

She glanced down at the pendant around her neck, then back to the man who stood before her. Yes, it was clear now, something delightfully mystifying had happened.

Unbothered by her question, Amal gestured to the opposite wall. "Here, this painting shows the weighing of the heart of the dead against the feather of truth."

The image of a giant scale, manned by a jackal-headed god, spanned much of the center of the wall. A rather anatomically correct heart sat on one side opposite a large feather, the bowls of the scale perfectly balanced.

"It's how we are judged worthy of the next life," Amal said simply.

"And are you?" Geraldine asked, not unkindly.

He looked at his feet without answering, which felt like answer enough.

"I'm sorry if I've offended you," Geraldine said, resting her hand on his shoulder in apology. "I want to understand. Is this...your pyramid?" She wasn't sure how else to phrase the question. "Are these writings about you?"

Amal thought for a moment before looking back at her. "Yes. And no." He took a breath before elaborating. "Some of the stories are about all of us, even you. Instructions on the journey, guidelines for the many tasks that lie ahead."

"And the others?"

"They tell stories of great accomplishments across the dynasty: conquering kings, prosperous kingdoms, bountiful harvests, the building of grand cities," Amal explained as they continued walking. "But none of them are mine."

A pang of understanding clenched Geraldine's heart. She knew the feeling well, watching the people around her accomplish a great many things, while she faded into oblivion. Still, she tried to reassure the king. "Every person impacts their world in *some* way."

She certainly hoped this was true. She had long believed her life could have a positive influence on others, and yet as she neared the end of hers, she found it more and more difficult to recall any lasting difference she'd made anywhere.

"You must have accomplished some things in your life worth

being remembered for," she prompted, before realizing she was wary of the man's answer. What would it mean for an insignificant person like her if this pharaoh, this king, said no?

Almost imperceptibly, Amal shook his head. "By the standard of building great palaces and temples, not so. I did not lead great battles, nor defend from invaders, nor guide my kingdom through strife. We were prosperous, we were safe. I kept the peace, but that is all."

"Peace is worth far more than you would think," Geraldine said. "You should be proud of that. We are still waiting for peace, even in my day."

"It doesn't feel like enough," Amal said. "I was remembered for a time, and then quickly forgotten in the wake of kings far greater than I. My whole life I strived to leave some kind of legacy, some mark on history, but there's nothing more to tell."

The next corner led them into a cavernous room, in which Geraldine's meager light did little to illuminate more than a meter or so in any direction. They came to a stop beside a wide stone pillar, carved deep with hundreds of cartouches: a list of past kings that must have spanned centuries. Amal's sad gaze trailed up the length of the column. "The world has forgotten me."

Geraldine and Amal stood for a while, staring at the pillar which seemed to stretch endlessly upward. Without the scuff of their feet against stone, the room amplified their very breaths.

"Will the world forget me, too?" she asked quietly. "I've done nothing close to the feats you've described."

Amal thought for a moment. "Long ago, I asked one of the high priests to prophesy the future of the kingdom, my future. All he told me was that everything would come to ruin."

"That is not very encouraging," she said.

"It isn't," Amal laughed lightly in agreement.

"Prophecies though," Geraldine said, shaking her finger toward the pharaoh, "they often don't mean what they seem on the surface."

"How so?"

"Well, I suppose everything is lost to time at some point," Geraldine said. She thought about the structure surrounding them, how long it had stood against thousands of storms like the one that now raged outside. "Eventually, even the stars will burn out."

Amal considered this as he looked around the chamber. He led her a few steps toward another painted scene, their footsteps echoing against stone, the emptiness of the room unable to swallow the sound. "This tomb," he said. "It used to be full of treasures, items the kings had amassed in their lifetime, gifts for the gods, tools for the journey. Raiders and robbers stripped it bare centuries ago."

Geraldine squinted at the images adorning the wall. A king sat on a throne above thousands of people, distributing food and goods to his subjects. Farmers tended to crops, priests made offerings in temples, and a gang of hunters stalked their prey.

"All that remains are their stories," she said. "It took centuries just to decipher them, and even these are being worn away by the sand and sun and heat."

"Maybe grand stories of our achievements aren't the ones that matter," posited Amal.

She nodded. She liked the sound of that. "Maybe so. Maybe our legacies lie in the little moments, the love we share with our family, and the companionship of our friends."

"Perhaps one friend is enough to be remembered by," Amal said with a smile. He linked their arms together and surveyed the large chamber again. "If all we have built in this world will come to ruin, we must strive to build the things time cannot erase."

Geraldine felt a sort of lightness in her chest, like a weight that had settled there for decades had finally been removed.

"Come, I believe we are almost there," said Amal. He led her out of the empty room, down yet another hall that grew marginally brighter with each step. They made one final turn. Against the wall at the end of the next passageway, a thin ray of sunlight beamed against the stone.

"What do we do now?" she asked.

Amal read from the walls surrounding them once more, taking

slow steps down the hall as he translated. *"Pure one, assume thy throne in the boat of Ra, that you may sail the sky, that you may mount above the far-off ways, that you may sail with the imperishable stars."*[3]

"What does that mean?" Geraldine asked. "The imperishable stars?"

"They are the central stars, the ones which never set. I am meant to take my place among them, to lead them across the sky." Amal looked longingly toward the light that shone into the hall before he continued interpreting the hieroglyphs. *"There is no god who has become a star without a companion."* Amal paused their walk briefly, and looked at Geraldine. "Shall I be your companion?"[4]

"I'd like that," said Geraldine. She looked down at her sand-dusted shoes, then back to Amal. They had reached the end of the long hall, the bright desert sun casting a rectangle of light through the open entryway.

The king smiled at her. "I will remember you, and you will remember me."

"I suppose this is where we are meant to end," said Geraldine, gesturing to the entrance.

She looked out into the daylight and saw not the stairs she had descended into the pyramid, but a vast field of green, swaying papyrus plants. The sun was shining, and any trace of the dust storm had vanished.

"I will remember you, and you will remember me," repeated Geraldine.

"I will," Amal vowed.

They stepped out into the light, and the Great King Sekhemwyhotep and Geraldine—may they live, prosper, and be well

---

3. *The Pyramid Texts,* Utterance 513; ancient Egyptian funerary texts inscribed on various pyramids and sarcophagi during the Old Kingdom (2649-2130 BC).
4. *The Pyramid Texts of Unas,* Utterance 215; the ancient Egyptian funerary text inscribed on the South wall of the sarcophagus chamber in the step pyramid at Saqqarah.

—walked beside one another across the field of reeds, no longer alone, no longer forgotten.

125

Story 9

The Blue Mantle

Gwendalina K.K. Buller

Our Lady spoke in the Polish language. And Krzysia would too if she had a tongue. A whole one at least.

But she hadn't since the stormy night two years ago, when a big wave fell on the deck. The captain of the ship said (in French with a very heavy Italian accent) that it was a miracle she wasn't swept away into the depths of the sea. Well, her whole body hadn't. But half of her tongue had been.

As if the world that rarely forgave punished her for lying.

She told Papa she wouldn't leave her hammock. But once he had fallen asleep, she had. She just wanted to see the lightning and the waves...she had never seen a seastorm before!

Well, she tasted blood mixed with salt instead. She bit her tongue way too hard. And well, too late, considering the fact that it was only after the lie escaped her lips and did its evil.

Now, on this new voyage, she could only watch and listen. Dark clouds gathered in the horizon, flying low above the waves as if they were black dragons trying to catch a fish. Navy water roared and kept dancing as a pagan warrior after a battle. Every now and then, swift snakes of lightning fell down, trying to reach water. The storm didn't reach the ship yet, but was visible.

It wasn't that unique in itself, but the whole journey was a different kind than any else Krzysia had been on. Ever since she could remember, her family was always running away from something. Death most of the time. *Kostucha*[1] liked to dress in different garments, whether a secret police uniform or the suit of an engineer who said there was no need for new workers, but nonetheless, she always seemed to be on the hunt for Majewscy. Once she caught their trail, they had to leave. That's how it was before.

Today they didn't run from the storm, but the ship sailed right into it. Pan Majewski hoped that on the other side there would be a completely clear sky, unlike the clouds that kept them in the shadows for so long. He and Krzysia were supposed to come back to their country.

They heard that the Queen of Poland came back to her people. And so they sailed to Her. To seek Her protection.

Even if they weren't sure if She actually did. They only heard rumours about apparitions of Our Lady somewhere...was it Warmia? Yes, it had to be. And to Krzysia's father it was all worth risking even the dangers of a storm, metaphorical or literal.

Pan Majewski walked over to his ten-year-old daughter and put his hand on her shoulder.

"You better hide under the deck soon, *jejmościanko*[2]."

She nodded and looked up at him. He smiled at her weakly. She took his hand and started walking towards the entrance to the subdeck.

They didn't need to go a long way. They weren't rich passengers. They slept in a room with the cargo that the ship carried. It wasn't the big storeroom—no one would let them in there—but a smaller one

---

1. Kostucha is a name for the personification of Death in Polish folklore, similar to the Grim Reaper.
2. A honorific used towards Polish noblewomen, but changed in a hypocoristic way to create a pet name.

with a few things too heavy to carry out by two people and enough space for two to sleep. This room was in front of stairs that led down from the deck.

"You should learn to go to sleep without holding my hand," Pan Majewski sighed as they entered their current shelter.

Krzysia took the hammock from one of the big boxes with something that smelled like tons of spices, giving her papa a side eye. The aroma was so strong it was hard not to suffocate. Even a small candle hanging in a lantern above flickered as if it felt nauseated.

The girl tried to hang up her hammock herself to show her father her annoyance, but he helped her anyway.

He was right. In the past she had been the complete opposite of what she became recently. She hadn't held his hand on their journey to Scotland. Or to Spain, to France, to Canada two years ago. Back then, she didn't feel the need to. Even as they passed the border of two invaders of their country, Russia and Austria, when Papa had to escape after Russians found out he printed old Polish books and wanted to send him to Siberia or worse.

She didn't even think of holding father's hand after he sat with red eyes, hugging mother's Rosary to his heart when her body got buried in a small cemetery in cold, Scottish ground, without any tree or a rock that would let an exile carve whimsy Polish letters into it.

Only recently, she learned to take his hand into hers. Now, disgraced by some of the people in nobility, he worked anywhere he could to feed his little daughter without thinking if the job was proper for a nobleman or not. Only since their voyage to Canada had she understood that she didn't deserve her father's sacrifices.

Sometimes she wondered if their nation, which Pan Majewski loved so much—he gave up everything for it—was maybe unworthy of his love as well. He was mistaken when it came to Krzysia; why wouldn't he be about Poland, then?

She still couldn't let go of his hand at night. Not because she was scared of him leaving her, but rather of hurting him again. Since she lost half of her tongue, he didn't have anyone from whom he could hear a word in the language for which he was ready to go into exile.

Pan Majewski bound himself with a rope to a wall and laid himself next to her hammock on the floor as he always did. People mocked him for treating his ten-year-old like a baby, but he never scolded her for her childishness. Until now at least.

"If Aunt Marianka will be able to take you in, I can hide in the convent for a few days, but not any longer," he continued, "and even then I can't be with you in the house of your aunt when you're asleep. Just like Russians, Prussians very much dislike Polish nationalists."

She was relieved she couldn't answer him. She didn't have to argue about it, nor surrender. She only squeezed his hand.

She needed him now. She wasn't able to see the light of tomorrow morning's sun through the storm clouds like her papa always seemed to do. This whole journey seemed to her like a great waste of effort and resources, but he claimed it was vital and worth any struggle. All because of some rumours.

She didn't know how Pan Majewski got to know about apparitions of Our Lady in Gietrzwałd. But somehow he could always find beautiful stories, even if it seemed impossible. Well, maybe the fact that he himself didn't accept the existence of the word "impossible" had something to do with it.

Father believed that if the Mother of God Herself spoke Polish and didn't let this language die out, but instead cultivated it through miracles, then maybe a time of mercy for Poland had finally come.

He worked for more than a year to be able to get his daughter to the place sanctified by Our Lady. He was sure that Krzysia could be healed if only they both came to Gietrzwałd and asked Mary, Queen of Poland, to grant this grace.

Krzysia was terrified of what would happen if they got there. She had been justly punished. She didn't see why she should be granted healing. Even now she couldn't help but hold her papa's hand when she slept, forcing him to sleep in a very uncomfortable position.

But she was so scared.

The hammock swung more and more frantically, not being able to find rest just like Krzysia's mind. Ironic. She couldn't talk, but in her mind she went on and on monologuing like characters from the play *Ksiądz Marek*,[3] a copy of which Papa always carried with him. He told her that normally these monologues would be said out loud by actors in a theatre.

Once she dreamt of experiencing such a spectacle. Now she preferred the characters' monologues staying silent. Quiet but true. It helped her feel less alone.

"I'm serious, *jejmościanko*." Pan Majewski jiggled the hand of his daughter between his as the hammock kept swaying from side to side. "One day when you're old and married, you'll be able to find me somewhere. But it will be better for you to stay with Aunt Marianka till that day. It's been cruel enough to wander with you all this time from one poor and freezing room to another. But after this journey I won't be able to give you even such luxuries. And Aunt Marianka has a house, money. And she lives among our people on our land."

Krzysia knew that her aunt had good intentions when she wrote a letter to Pan Majewski, wishing to take under her care the daughter of her deceased sister. Krzysia still felt as if she had been hurt by this arrangement. Papa would never let his little *jejmościanka* be taken away from him before. But after Krzysia lost the ability to speak, he was ready to even lose her as long as she'd be healed and safe.

So it all came back again to this: everything was Krzysia's own fault.

"Jejmościanko?"

She tilted on her side and sunk her vision in the calm, gray sea of her papa's eyes.

"You understand what I'm saying?"

She sighed, but nodded.

---

3.   A drama written by Juliusz Słowacki. It tells the story of Father Marek who was a member of Bar Confederation which is considered by some as the first Polish national uprising.

Now he would stand up and walk away, find himself a hammock, and sleep soundly as he deserved. And she'd stay alone, as she deserved.

But his body didn't move. Only the corners of his mouth lifted up in a gentle smile. A tear fell from Krzysia's eyes onto his cheek.

"Oh no, don't cry, *jejmościanko*," Pan Majewski said with concern, standing up. He leaned over and took her in his arms, intending to hold her to his heart. "I'll miss you too, but..."

He didn't get a chance to finish. A sudden shake caused Krzysia to fall on the floor. Thanks to the rope, they didn't pitch against the tilting side of the ship, only hit the wall and got showered by some loose objects. Sometimes things like this happened in times of storm. Papa explained to Krzysia once that big enough waves pushed ships onto their sides.

This time it felt a bit different, though. Before her father could get up and help Krzysia to crawl back into her hammock, the whole ship quivered again, even harder, as if it was a house in the middle of an earthquake. Krzysia felt as if her brain and guts tried to rip her skin and bones apart as the side of the ship suddenly became the floor. Papa gripped her tightly to keep her from rolling.

The ship wobbled, causing everything in the room to dance, jump and fall from one side to the other as if they were playing tag. Then a stream of furniture ran down the floor heedless of the two passengers.

Pan Majewski tried to protect his daughter with his own body, but Krzysia still got hit on the head by the corner of a table top. It was quite rotten and she heard it falling apart not long after it passed her, but its edge was still sharp and it cut the girl's skin, causing a trickle of blood to run down the side of her head. A few wooden boxes tumbled against her legs.

The sudden pain and fright filled her hurting head with images of her body covered with millions of black bruises. She felt as if it was, even though it probably wasn't. The ship seemed to slowly lean onto its side more and more, causing more objects to move.

Something freezing reached for her head from above. It ran down her body, cooling down the hot blood that flew from the cut skin. Even though it was cold, it made her wound burn even more.

Krzysia's heart came to her throat.

Seawater.

"The ship is sinking!"

She wasn't sure if the scream came out of the throat of her father, another passenger, sailor, all of them together or just her horrified imagination. But it tore through her conscience like lightning through the sky.

She would have probably just lain there terrified and let the sea slowly cover her with its icy shroud, but her father had other plans. He kept her close with his one hand, not letting her be swept away, as he tried to stand up. The floor kept shaking, so he didn't get to his feet, but climbed up along the rope on his knees, trying to reach the wall. Krzysia started crawling next to him, trying to be less of a burden.

When they reached the wall, Majewski grabbed a hook pinned in the wall and looked at his daughter.

"Can you bind yourself to this rope?"

She nodded shakily and started. In the meantime he held her, but also searched for something in the flickering light of the lantern hanging above.

When she finished, she nudged him with her elbow. He quickly looked at her and then at the knot.

"It should work out fine," he said, after checking it. "Now we need to find—"

The door opened and a wave drifted in. The lantern's light finally went out. Krzysia heard a sequence of closer and closer splashes.

"What are you two waiting for? I'm not going to carry you out, so get going!" a young sailor snapped in English. "Out! Now! Before the life boats start to float away!"

"We need a moment," hissed pan Majewski through clenched teeth as he seemed to search the water around them frantically. At least the ripples of water suggested so. "I have to..."

"There's no moment to spare!" the sailor interrupted him. "There's a big hole in the magazine, almost next door to you. If you don't get out now, water will soon bury you here. And with this wind it's also hard to keep life boats ready for laggards. Get out!"

"But..."

Pan Majewski tried to argue again, but the sailor wouldn't let him.

"Get. Out. Now."

Sounds of splashing water communicated to Krzysia that the sailor wasn't planning to help them. The next big wave of ice cold water washed over her legs. From the door that the sailor left open a faint light came in and disappeared. Probably the more rational sailors or more lucky passengers carried some kind of lanterns as they evacuated the ship.

Krzysia looked up at her father, taking advantage of the flickering light. A frown of concern clouded Papa's face. She wasn't sure why. She had almost never seen fear on his face. But then, though they traveled on many ships, none of those sank until today.

They climbed up the stairs that looked like a small waterfall now. It wasn't easy. Two currents, one coming from the magazine down the ship and one from the water falling from the deck above, tried to keep them in a whirlpool. It was especially hard for Krzysia. She couldn't rely on her father's help that much, as Pan Majewski struggled himself to climb up. She had to make an effort to not be a complete obstacle to him. But even if her body didn't hurt as much as before, the cold that made her whole body tremble uncontrollably and her limbs, pathetically weak, didn't help. Water splashing into her face and filling her nose wasn't making anything easier.

Finally, a cold wind blew against her face. Soon she found herself above deck. The floor shook and was again swamped by gigantic waves. The ship trembled under the pressure of the troubled sea which tried to toss it around as if it was playing with a ball.

In the light of lightning and flickering of small lanterns, Krzysia noticed that other people gathered on the less sunken side of the ship and were helped into small lifeboats.

Two sailors who helped the other few passengers called out, "Here!"

Pan Majewski hesitated and looked behind him. He started untying the rope that held him and Krzysia together.

"*Jejmościanko*, go to them. I'll be there in a moment. I just have to find our luggage. Go."

The rope fell to the ground just before the shadow of a wave so big a shriek tore through Krzysia's throat, the first in a long time. It was not only scared, but a shrill shriek as well, alarming almost as much as the fierce roars of the sea, wordless and strange to her ears. Water came falling down too swiftly, yet painfully slowly as if it found joy in looking deeply into black, wide eyes of a small girl shaking from fear and cold.

But before it could swallow her, she was caught and hidden in the arms of her papa. She felt warmer for a second as if she got close to the last spark of the fire.

Then the roaring sea hit. Even though she kept them shut, her eyes burned; even though she didn't breathe in, she felt her lungs get stuffed with heavy coldness; even though her limbs seemed firm, water played with them as with a puppet.

Yet Papa held her through it all. She felt like ages passed before her head reached the surface of the water. And even then, before she could take a breath, the ocean's hands pushed her again into the depths with unimaginable force.

There was too much water everywhere and no air! Mostly no light, but when a bolt struck she was blinded and didn't know where to swim. She felt lost. Completely.

As much as desperation gave her strength to reach the surface of the water once in a while, she discovered to her even greater fright that it became harder with every try. Her hands and legs first moved too slow and then failed to move at all. She couldn't breathe. She couldn't move. She couldn't even think anymore.

Krzysia couldn't tell if she was swimming or not. It seemed to her that she was, but she couldn't feel her limbs. She tried to swim again. But her whole body felt more and more heavy and frozen. Telling what was only her imagination and what was not became harder and harder. Reality became strange and scary to her hazy mind. She didn't know how through all of the noise of the sea and storm her ears caught her papa's breaking whispers.

"Queen... of... Poland... pray... for... us..."

Maybe she only dreamt that.

* * *

She woke up not feeling cold nor drowning. She tried to hold on to that fact. It brought her closer to the surface of consciousness when the pain only pushed her deeper into the unresting darkness of nightmares.

She felt a bit similar to a time when Mama paid for her to ride a cheap carousel. Her head was spinning and spinning, and hurting too...and her skin seemed to be torn everywhere, and her whole body felt at the same time as if it was both burning and cold from within, and...

She didn't feel like she was freezing though. No. She felt quite warm. Warmer than in the room without windows where she had lived with her papa. The curtains of her eyelids seemed less black than normal. But it all was pleasant, the pain and the fright easing when she held onto the feeling of comfort.

Could she be in Heaven? Even after everything she had caused? Or maybe Purgatory was just less scary than everyone had told her?

She heard a crackling of fire and some kind of ringing, as if of lazy bells. No, definitely Purgatory, if not the first circle of hell.

She tried to open her eyes, but the eyelids seemed too heavy to lift. Another sound caught her attention.

Two voices whispered words unfamiliar to her. It felt like they were trying to speak Polish, but instead of doing that like Papa and

Mama who spoke with such melodic tones, the voices grunted every word with harshness. Sometimes even added strange phrases that weren't part of Polish, and sounded even more like snarling.

This had to be a place of punishment for liars.

Krzysia tried to curl up, but her body burned with pain, causing her to freeze. She mewled quietly from hurt and fear. Couldn't she talk with God before she got sent here?

She'd tell Him how much she missed Mama. And that Papa would miss her after getting to Heaven if she couldn't follow. And that she was very sorry. And that she knew she was evil, but she just couldn't keep up being good; she didn't have the strength.

God was loving. He'd listen. He wouldn't want Papa to be unhappy. Oh, if they only let her speak with Him!

"*Jejmościanko?*"

She opened her eyes widely.

Above her there was a yellow wooden ceiling covered with black stains and spider webs.

The shaky whisper of Papa's voice came somewhere from her left. She tried to turn, but her body was too heavy.

So she couldn't be dead. Papa wouldn't go anywhere less than Heaven among God's Troops, servants of Mary. And this place definitely wasn't the resting place of Polish Saints. No one sang, nor joked. Plus, she felt pain. And in Heaven there should be no pain, right?

A shadow covered her. A woman with tired, green eyes and a warm frown on her face touched Krzysia's forehead.

"She still hassa fev'r," she sighed.

She smiled a little. In a different way than Krzysia's mother used to, but somehow the gesture brought to the girl's heart a bit of similar peace. The lady started in a soft tone speaking, but with the same strange, harsh manner and she used so many words unknown to Krzysia that the girl couldn't understand anything.

But she knew that both she and Papa were in the hands of good people. When they were supposed to be dead. How strange.

* * *

Their hosts carried the name of Fręceks. They were a good-hearted and hardworking fishermen family. Though Krzysia had a hard time communicating with them as they spoke *gwara*[4] with influences of German (as Papa explained to her), she soon developed lots of sympathy for Pan Maciej, Pani Asia and their three children.

Those three were younger than her, but old enough for them to all play together. As she grew stronger, they treated her more and more like their friend and wanted to show her and teach her everything. She was very happy spending time with her playmates, but her heart ached when she had to stay away from her papa.

Pan Majewski didn't feel better. His arm had been injured and gangrene had seeped into the wound. He seemed weaker and weaker every day. All he said when he was able, and when Krzysia wasn't near, was her name.

She sat next to his bed by the wall as long as Pani Asia let her. The good woman didn't allow Krzysia to spend her whole time by her papa's side. She was strict about girl's rest and time in the fresh air, saying something like, "little Issa still weak."

Krzysia followed the woman's orders. Most of the time. One day when the couple went to do something with Fręcek's boat and the children played outside, Krzysia meant to join them, but heard her papa's calling her.

"Krzysiu... Krzysiu..."

She hastened to his side. Kneeling down, she took his hand in hers. She kissed it to show him she was there. Most of the time he calmed down a little after she assured him she was near. Only then he fell asleep.

But now he looked up at her instead. Krzysia's heart raced with joy. His eyes looked way less foggy than in the past two weeks. He seemed very tired, but conscious. He actually looked at her and

---

4. A dialect.

recognised her. His face wasn't as red. He had started coming back to health.

"*Jejmościanko?*" he whispered. Krzysia kissed his cheek. She didn't know how to show him that yes, she was there. She hugged him delicately.

He smiled weakly, "I see you...I...I just want to tell you something...but I can't find words..."

Krzysia caressed his cheek. She didn't need him to find the right words. The fact that he talked to her was enough.

"Back on the ship...I wanted to go back for our documents, fake ones." He grimaced. "I thought I lost you when this wave took you away...I'm sorry. Maybe we both would be safe and sound if I wouldn't worry so much about them. If I didn't untie the rope...you wouldn't be washed away, I wouldn't have had to jump after you and nothing would look as it does now."

She shook her head. It was more than obvious that he had something very important on his mind back then. She knew he would never put anything above his family's wellbeing. Everything just happened too fast.

"But on the other hand, if we hadn't had them in the seaport, we would've been sent back where we came from...or worse. If we had them now, we'd be able to travel almost safely." He coughed. He still felt the need to explain himself. Didn't she show well enough that she didn't blame him at all? "And yes...that's the problem. Now we have none. You at least. Because I might not need them anymore."

Krzysia frowned.

"Don't be surprised, please. I feel that I won't be able to stay with you for much longer." Tears filled his eyes. He lifted his shaking hand and rested it on Krzysia's cheek. "I don't want to leave my little *jejmościanka*, I don't want to..."

The despair in his voice pierced through the girl's heart like a bullet. She burst out crying. So this was the end. Her papa swallowed and tried to *otrzeć* her tears with his shaking thumb.

"I don't want to leave you," he repeated. "But because I doubted, this fate has fallen upon me. But listen, don't follow my mistake. Do you understand?"

She shook her head. His eyes softened.

"I need to leave, but you're not staying here alone," he whispered. "Never. Remember. We are Polish people. We are children of God and of Our Lady. She saved you, *jejmościanko*. I begged her as waves tried to bury me to rescue my child, and She did. Now I beg Her to carry you through this life and keep you under Her mantle always. She has a gentle heart, and She always listens. She will be with you. And She'll bring you closer to God. And I promise you that when you'll let yourself be brought to Him, we'll meet again. Mama will be there too. In a blink of an eye. Moments, unpleasant ones, seem long, but they always pass. And there is no separation to people whose love is forever. Love is a strong rope that can never be cut, nor untied. We'll see each other again soon. And if God allows me, my soul will never leave yours, but guard it always. I love you, *Krzysiu*."

He looked her in the eyes. She wanted to scream that she loved him too, but couldn't.

"Remember, you're not alone," he said again. "If you ever feel lonely, look up at the sky, at the blue mantle. Just like the one with which Our Lady covers you if you want Her to take care of you. Always."

He raised his hand and blessed her by drawing a sign of Cross on her forehead just like he always did. It was so simple. Yet it felt more precious than the greatest treasure in the world.

He looked her in the eyes again. Neither of them could speak, but love was so clear it felt almost tangible. More real than most flowery words could describe, as if stars shone in the two pairs of eyes.

Suddenly though, the light in Pan Majewski's eyes dimmed as a shadow filled them. His hand fell from her face like a toy with which a child felt bored. Krzysia kept crying quietly. But as pathetic as it all looked, she didn't fall into despair.

She felt that God would grant her papa's wish. Now she'd never let go of Papa's hand. And he was right. Terrible things were only mere moments.

And Our Lady came to take care of Poland, even if it was guilty of its own fall. She could also, with Her love, lift up Krzysia. Nothing was really lost if there was love.

The girl curled up by her papa's side and put her head on his heart. It wasn't beating. But one day it would again. She only had to wait.

"A silent girl stood for thirteen whole days by a small grave labeled Józef Majewski," they said. "She was his daughter, lost the ability to speak after his death, probably. Poor child. She had to write his name on paper so *proboszcz*[5] would know whom he'd bury. And after these thirteen days she just left. Strange story."

"Did you hear about a little silent pilgrim? She's a girl, not older than your daughter. No one knows who her parents are! Definitely not any of my sisters. We wouldn't let a child wander around and play a beggar. Why is she called a pilgrim? She stays longer by every cross on the road and looks at it with fondness, forgetting the world around her. Maybe she's a little bit mad."

Krzysia finally reached Gietrzwałd. It was a small village. Morning sun painted it with gold on the thatched roofs of the white houses and green on the fields behind them. Along the road, poppies red as

---

5. Polish name for a parish priest.

blood and cornflowers blue as the night sky bathed in the rays of light, just as everywhere in this land. But somehow exceptionally beautiful.

She couldn't say if it was the small meadows, embroidered with rainbow colours behind, or the softly singing high trees in the village that made it so special. But she knew it was. Whispers of the wind told her they liked playing among the grass and leaves here.

But even if she didn't feel anything, the journey—as bitter as sometimes it had felt—was worth it. Papa had wanted to get her here so badly; she couldn't not come.

It was the best bet to look here for Aunt Marianka as well. After all, Majewscy were supposed to meet with her here at the church.

Obviously, Father was supposed to be there. This would make everything easier, because he knew his sister-in-law, and Krzysia didn't really remember her aunt at all. The girl wasn't sure how she could introduce herself when she would meet Pani Marianka. But she hoped that maybe her aunt would recognize her.

If she journeyed here with Father alive and well as planned, they would get to Gietrzwałd faster too. They were supposed to meet with Krzysia's aunt a while ago. But Papa wasn't here, and she couldn't arrive in Gietrzwałd earlier. So she tried to hope that her aunt hadn't left the neighborhood yet.

No matter what would happen though, Krzysia'd somehow survive. Of that she was sure. She came to her Queen and Mother.

She walked to where a small chapel stood next to a maple tree, just before the village. People gathered for prayer here. After saying a rosary with everyone else, she stood up and contemplated the figure of Our Lady. Her face was so gentle and kind... just as father described to Krzysia.

A girl, not much older than Krzysia came over and nudged the other girl with her elbow.

"Hi!" she smiled. "What's your name?"

Krzysia only smiled back. She wasn't sure what to do.

"You're a shy one, eh?" the girl rolled her eyes. "Don't worry. I'm your friend! Where are your parents? Are you alone? Did you come from a faraway village? I'm from here. I know Basia, the visionary, you know? But I'll tell you about it later maybe. We'll have dinner soon in my house, and my mama has said that you can join us if you want."

Krzysia would be very happy to answer all of these questions. But she couldn't. It didn't feel right. Father had such a strong faith that she'd get healed if she travelled to Gietrzwałd... and nothing happened. She felt as if nothing had changed. There was still no tongue to form the sounds coming from her throat. She mumbled something, but it wasn't anything in any language known to man.

"What did you say?" the girl asked. "Sorry. I didn't understand."

She didn't notice Krzysia's condition. *Maybe that's for the better.* Majewska felt too tired for weird looks and concerned questions.

She was frustrated. She felt guilty for disappointing her papa, but also angry that the world turned out to not be as beautiful as he told her it was. Maybe she wasn't the biggest liar in the family after all.

"My mom really won't mind if you come over for dinner, don't worry," the girl repeated.

Krzysia wasn't in the mood to join a happy family for dinner. She got an invitation, though, and turning it down without a reason wouldn't be polite.

She pondered for a moment what she should do. Her first responsibility was to try and find her aunt. She looked around. A few people still prayed in the place of the apparitions, but Majewska didn't see anyone similar in the face to her mother. Or any person who looked like a noble lady.

So her aunt wasn't here, at least not now. Even though it wasn't something unexpected, Krzysia still felt disappointment. Was the journey here a waste after all? Maybe Aunt wasn't even in the neighborhood anymore. Maybe Krzysia went this whole way for nothing.

The miracle that Papa expected didn't happen. Her aunt wasn't here. Krzysia only lost everything and didn't gain anything. It had all turned out even worse than she imagined. She almost laughed hysterically.

"So? Are you going?" the girl inquired.

With all of the strength she could find in herself, Krzysia just smiled and nodded.

"Great!" The girl grabbed Majewska's hand and pulled her towards one of the farmhouses. "My name is Rózia Sosnowska, by the way. What's your name? And where are you from?"

Oh no. This Rózia just has to keep going, doesn't she?

She tried to show Rózia she couldn't speak. She would prefer to just write it out on the dry ground, but this was impossible when Sosnowska just kept marching on, dragging her along. So Krzysia only pointed at her mouth and then shook her head a few times.

Rózia frowned. "Why won't you say anything? Are you a Prussian or what? Why did you come to the maple tree of Our Lady at all?"

Krzysia felt her heart squeezing. Papa would never let his identity and love for Mother of God not be known. She wished she could express her own.

She wanted to believe. She almost did! After all, whatever she'd thought in a moment of anger, she knew Papa couldn't be wrong.

I'm sorry I almost called you a liar. I'm sorry.

He couldn't be. Krzysia just didn't have enough faith, that was all. She shouldn't have waited for one specific miracle.

So many wonders have happened already. She was saved twice from the storm by Mother Mary. Our Lady filled her heart with hope and reminded her that She was always protecting her child through the last words of Papa. Now the Queen of Poland sent her a friend, so she wouldn't feel alone without Papa and her aunt.

All this time...

Krzysia looked up at the crystal sky for the moment—blue and calming, embroidered with a few white clouds. Beautiful Mantle of the most Blessed Mother who gave Her daughter so much.

Thank You...

Krzysia lowered her head and squeezed her eyes shut. Papa wasn't wrong. She understood now. Queen of Poland was still with

Her people. She took care of Krzysia. Through every smile, through every good word, through every soft heart that felt pity for the Silent Pilgrim as people called her.

"Hey. Are you alright?" Rózia nudged Krzysia's arm cautiously. "I mean, there's nothing wrong with being a Prussian, they can be kind too. You seem like a nice one. I just don't speak Prussian well, only my dad does, so er...if you don't understand, how do I explain it..."

Krzysia almost cried as she looked up at Sosnowska. If she could only explain everything...she knew the words she wanted to say. If she only could... if she could, she would say that...

"*Jestem Polką*.[6] I'm Krzysia Majewska, and I came back home to my Queen and Mother, to serve Her. If Our Lady comes to us Poles, to give us hope, we need to give back hope to Her," Krzysia thought out loud.

Out. Loud.

Tears filled her eyes. She jumped up and started laughing as she hadn't done in years. She danced around, leading confused Rózia after herself.

"Oh. I see. You're crazy," Sosnowska said.

Krzysia stopped. She blushed a little. It didn't hurt her when people thought of her as crazy. "I'm sorry for that," she said, wiping away her tears. "I just...felt so much joy. So much joy. Because..."

"Because?" Rózia raised an eyebrow.

Krzysia shrugged.

"Our Lady is...so good," she said.

"She is," Sosnowska nodded, smiling. "Realising that sometimes causes people to dance. Maybe there should be more of that. But anyway, come on." She took Krzysia by the arm and led towards the farmhouse. "You need to eat something. You look as if you haven't eaten in years!"

---

6. "I'm a Pole" in Polish.

Krzysia looked up at the sky. She felt that she wasn't smiling alone. Her parents also smiled.

She didn't see that yet. But she had seen the beautiful blue mantle of Our Lady above her, and so she knew that all of what her papa said was true. And even if the clouds gathered and covered it, the mantle still was above them. Krzysia was always hidden under it.

She only had to stay faithful.

Story 10

The Other Son

Elizabeth Ruda

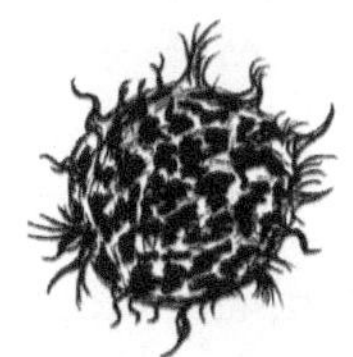

To most, this year's mission wasn't a once-in-a-lifetime experience. The sun would spray its unwanted plasma at thousands of miles per hour toward the Farian atmosphere again in twelve years—and the government would send scientists up to study its auroras. The star had done thus for generations, since the ancients spun sticks to start sacrificial fires, sending goats or wine up in smoke toward the light they thought housed gods. It had done it until now, when the people called the wonder a "coronal mass ejection," when its sacred flame was measured and its properties assessed, when the source of its radiance—plasma—was reined into orderly magnetic fields. The people of Faria had learned from the sun itself to wield and destroy with its power shadow, deadly cold, and the very pull of gravity beneath their feet. Any thought of spirits or souls? Up in smoke with the ancients' offerings. Yet there were some things plasma still could not completely subdue: starvation, disease, and the mind of one Lieutenant Meran.

Incomprehensibly, this year, Meran was going up to catch a god.

He did his job faithfully, as any soldier should. A *Farian* soldier, no less, would not be caught dead failing in his filial obligations, even if they primarily entailed filing and figuring. The numbers, the equations, the os and 1s of it all—these were air to him, necessary for the greater good and knowledge of his people. But his heart, his lifeblood —that was another matter. When the reedwork calmed, when his training for spaceflight granted a few spare moments in between lifting weights and fine-tuning his ship's gravity plating, he turned back to his notes on the Forefathers.

Underneath all his desk's filepads and reedpapers was a small, unassuming notebook, an extra from his academy days that had blended in well with others dedicated to logarithms and plasma burn triage. Here, though, at the Central Command base, it stood out, written in longhand, crinkled, stained, with pages torn and meticulously secured again with thread to the binding. It was nearly filled, but to him, especially today, its words barely brushed the depths of what he'd have to know. Parables were, of course, only marginally conducive to spaceflight. The personal encounters would theoretically be the most useful. He cracked open the spine.

His communicator let out a *brrreeen.*

"Lieutenant Meran." A small image of his superior saluted him. He flicked off the camera cover and silently returned the gesture. "Our solar probes are reporting pre-ejection magnetic buildup as anticipated. This CME is looking to be small, with about a week expected before its brunt hits planetside. Your observation of its trajectory from the exosphere should be unimpeded. That being said, I expect both to be worthy of note, given your own track record."

Meran bowed his head. "You honor me and the beloved around me, ma'am," he replied, routinely.

His superior smiled. "You are approved for launch at 2400. I expect to see you fully suited at 1200. No tardiness permitted."

"Your word is my duty." He glanced at the clock—1147. The launch wouldn't be for another twelve hours and thirteen minutes. "Respectfully, Colonel Lae—"

"As if you are ever tardy, Meran," she chuckled. "If preparations actually required 1200, you would have already been in the hangar bay."

"Yes, I would have." Meran's brow bent in confusion. Lae laughed again at this, only making it worse.

"Well, thankfully, we no longer rub sticks together to start engine fires, so your devotion there is unnecessary," she continued, and shook her head. "Speaking of devotion..."

Meran flinched, but only a hair.

"Refrain from antagonizing the rest of this crew with ghost stories."

"Colonel—"

Lae held up a hand. "Your beliefs are recognized. Reflect on the opportunity I have given you, and let that be enough for your gods."

"But they are your gods as well, Lae—"

Lae's gills flared. Meran shut his mouth. The colonel waited, then continued: "Your practice, as well as your participation, are privileges not appreciated by all my superiors. Understood?"

He stared blankly at the screen. After a moment, Lae relaxed. "You are free to respond."

Meran swallowed bile, then forced himself to salute. "Understood." Lae returned it, then disconnected.

Meran sighed, turning back to his desk, lowering his head into his pale blue hand.

Lae had suffered in her life just as he had. She knew what consolation the ancient ways were to him, and to others across generations, though few as of late. Why did she harass and reprimand him? So what if he read and prayed here and there on base? Spoke hard truths, especially to ensigns who needed to be taught of their vanities? Occasionally slipped reed pamphlets into flight-suit lockers? What truly mattered was restoring Faria to its former glory, namely, the glory that came from proper, worldwide worship, and the resulting mercy of its creators.

But he had gotten distracted. Right now, to Command, *that* was what mattered. The Forefather Aijhem emphasized obedience in his epistles...though he wrote in a world in which superiors too were faithful. Certainly such people could not have been so frivolous as to crack jokes at their inferiors' expense, especially while on duty...Still, if Faria was so divinely favored once, it could be again.

He'd continue to solve for how *after* he left the office.

The hours until launch slurred together. A preflight physical preceded a mental aptitude test, then a piloting competency review (each mildly insulting to Meran, but required). Then came low-gravity and zero-gravity performance tests, with dinner consumed *after*, not before. Meran's recitation of prayers and quintuple washing of hands before the meal brought stares, silent and prolonged.

Good, he thought. *Let them hear me, and know the hope they are lacking.*

At the bell, he and the other mission staff were funneled into a strategy briefing on hostile entity encounters. Meran was made to introduce himself in his role as mission defense—not that extrafariestrials had yet been confirmed to exist, but a high probability had been calculated decades back; the council had been selecting their insurance for this CME event, and, knowing his skill, Lae had slid Meran's file under the appropriate door. And even if he was a newer lieutenant, used to shooting down meteoroids, not monsters, his skill commanded respect. A respect he hoped could transfer to his outlook on the gods, in the eyes of his peers.

"We do not need another lecture on mathematical ghost hunting," the pilots groaned at him.

"Is there nothing more to life than numbers?" he pleaded from the podium. "Have you forgotten what gives it meaning? Do you not sense the gravity of the judging eye of Sof, whose wheeled chariot soon will carry him across our atmosphere—"

"Mythology was a required course in our academy studies," said some researcher in the back. It was a familiar voice, but the light glinted off her glasses in a way that hid her face; he wasn't sure if a rebuke would impact the right ears. He continued to entreat them, but, sensing the "important" part to be over, the officers left one by one for the locker room, with the mission captain giving him a sideways look on his way out. Meran scoffed them off, and he quickly buried his face again in his notebook.

He and the others had a last chance to call home while the week's worth of supplies were checked and rechecked, but he did not see a need to break his focus. His eyes streaked across one page, then the next, then the one after, his free hand switching between grasping the notebook and yanking the back of his boot up his calf. It was time he tried that prayer formula, the one prescribed for strength in battle. (Whether that would be against some alien force or his own cohort remained to be seen.) His gear in place and the room mostly empty, he mentally calculated the proper direction to be in alignment with the Aterish constellation at this hour, knelt down, and flipped to the page.

His eyes only stared ahead, unable to continue. Another gaze was burning into his neck.

He glanced over his shoulder.

"What do you think you are doing?" he and his adversary asked in unison. Meran grimaced. It *was* her in that meeting: that one statistics officer whose name he never bothered to remember. Said officer adjusted her glasses with a clearing of her throat.

"My question was three twenty-fifths of a second sooner," she said.

His eyes narrowed. "I think I am preparing."

"Ah. I think I am reprimanding my colleague."

"And what is the nature of the offense?"

"Ignoring duty to pursue frivolous matters."

He rose to his feet (a bit too quickly for proper decorum). "I could say much the same."

"Yet words do not inherently belie truth. Such is the first lesson of semantics."

Meran's face flushed a bit purple. "You—every time I am minding a higher purpose, you somehow find the means to appear over my shoulder and contradict it. A purpose that was prescribed for *all* Farians from of old, may it be noted—"

"And yet to do so forgets our purpose as officers."

"Pray tell."

"You have already made lieutenant and require reminding?" Her expression was flat, and she clasped her hands behind her back. "Our *higher purpose* is to pursue knowledge, and, in doing so, to promote our people's advancement and evolution in an *efficient* manner, as has been done *from of old*, from the wheel to the starship." She held up a hand as Meran began to reply. "Mere thoughts and comforts do not change make. Action must supersede."

Meran sputtered, incredulous. "I do not do all of this for *feeling!* I pray and preach for—"

"The satisfaction of saying *you* have prayed and preached."

"What—what is *that* supposed to mean?"

The light again passed over her eyes. "The semantics are straight-forward."

Meran was dumbstruck. Once he regained his composure, he stepped over the bench toward her, thrusting his notes at her. "You—you insult me. You undermine your spiritual duty and waste prepara-tion time in—"

"I am trying to save all of us time, Lieutenant. Staff conversations with you are on average 32.27% longer than the prescribed length because you continually bring up your nonexistent deities and how we will all burn in the plasma flames for believing in observed reality. If they did exist, I should like to study their makeup myself; yet as it stands now, there are no gods. Efficiency must be kept in mind. Please, consider your conduct. May Faria be honored by your flight."

Meran stared at her. "May...Faria be honored by your flight," he managed to choke out, and the officer promptly left for the hangar.

How dare she say I do this for me.

It had been recorded, first by the great father Eijan, that the gods rode in a flaming chariot out across the skies. As the gods were true Gods, the beasts that pulled them were true Beasts from within the heart of the sun, and could not be fully tamed for long. This ride was meant to sate them. Their burning hooves had already scorched craters into Faria's moons, the three satellites pale white with the ash; the surface of the new world, full of the gods' Beloved, could not be suffered to bear the same.

The father Islian expounded upon this, recording a great battle between the driving god, Sof, and an unfaithful king. The king had turned the land's shrines into meeting-halls, full of feasting and sin, and was warned toward repentance. Yet, instead, the king had his rebuker trampled underfoot. Sof, hearing of this, rode out early, before he was to bring the sun that day, and sentenced the king to a similar death, though in fire—the crater range of Motonai around the world's equator remains a testament to this. But, seeing the destruction wrought, Sof pulled back on the reins, and sent cooling waters over the course of the skies. Thus, when the beasts ride again, waves and waves of color ripple over the surface of the world, reminding mortals that they are Beloved, and would never be so crushed again.

An alternate, transcending view was given by Jiuhnan, in a much later work: the chariot, Sof, and the beasts were the force of creation itself; the gods one intangible Being. But Jiuhnan died before he could explain his abstract symbols—a sheaf, a bowl, a circle.

Meran chewed on these stories as he taxied into formation, half-glancing at the small statuette of a feline wobbling atop his navigational controls. It had once been a light orange in color, but since was stained with ash. The stories comforted him. They were familiar, rote.

"It was the only possession we could recover from your room at the shrine, young Meran."

He didn't want to think about that.

"What of my family?" he asked.

The couple who would take him in shook their heads.

"I am sorry. We will bridge the gap they have left behind."

It was right, he begrudgingly replied to the memory, that his new family had never promised to *fill* that gap. Nothing on this world could.

They had told him it had been an accident. An overturned votive lamp, ornate curtains lingering just a bit too close. But the wavering lights in the sky told him differently: it was a judgement. A reckoning on all the beloved of Faria. Their devotion had lost its purity.

Over the next twelve years, Meran had kept his routines as well as he could remember them, and kept them strictly, so that he wouldn't forget any further. The shrine was rebuilt, for purposes of historical preservation, and it was only right that he took on its upkeep. He kept the visitors' areas clean, even when there were no visitors to respect. He found no excuse not to scrub. No excuse not to pray. He would show the gods there was no need for further wrath.

This structure kept him sane, he felt, and prepared him for the rigors of the Farian military. He couldn't fathom how the rest of the world seemed content to float by as cogs and pegs in the machine. How they must dry their tears with microchips. There was *peace* in the faith, in the tradition, in the knowledge that despite everything, the emptiness, the loss, one was not alone. A purpose greater than any crafted by mortals was already given, could be fought for, and won. *Why* could his comrades look, and not see? Listen to his heart's pleadings, and not hear? Calculate, but only count mere echoes of the truth?

And why would the gods still not speak to him when he cried out?

"*Research squadron cleared for launch.*"

After a good few hours, once the small fleet had halted near their observation buoy, the mission captain's voice crackled over the radio. "Confirm status."

"Port defense ready," Meran replied, powering down thrusters.

"Starboard defense ready."

"Research vessels, ready?"

"*Rael*, ready."

"*Minja*, ready."

The rest of the confirmations faded into chatter as Meran stared out at the stars. Little pinpricks, thousands and thousands of them, like salt across a tablecloth of black. Shortly—*finally*—his radar blipped.

"Coronal mass ejection in progress."

An arc of fire blossomed from the sun.

Orange, gold, and white danced across Meran's widened eyes. Light pulsing, rippling, gushing across the cloth like spilled wine, its glow lapping against the researchers' hulls. The CME was still millions upon millions of miles away, but he could see the crests of the wave, the places where plasma curled and peeled off into wisps, with the gaps of black they left behind. The chatter restarted, newly tense.

"Sir—ejection velocity increasing exponentially. Size also increasing. These—these phenomena have never before been recorded..."

"Fascinating," replied the captain. "Recommended actions?"

"Its magnetic field will hit us sooner than expect—disrupt our—return—base—"

"Captain to *Minja*, over—*Minja*, do you—over—"

Loud crackling filled Meran's headset until it was all he could hear—he ripped off his headphones, trying to stop his ears' ringing. His engines whirred on and off and on again while his cabin lights flickered like the stars outside. For all of Central's precautions, the whole squadron was in the same state, and the plasma storm, incomprehensibly, would envelop them in a matter of minutes. Meran's hands locked up. Their ships were not meant to withstand that kind of heat. But despite that, now how was he supposed to—

The arc flashed. The storm's flames seemed to bend, glistening off of heads, off proud, shining helmets, glittering pauldrons, and snorting, wild, horselike creatures, daring not to even singe a strange, holy force now charging through the darkness.

Meran pressed a hand against his viewport, pulse ricocheting through his fingers.

This would be his only chance.

He recalibrated his engines' plasma flow, rerouted power to them from the environmental systems. The engines whirred back to stability.

Meran shot into the storm.

Despite his experience, Meran's hearts froze with every unmitigated smack of solar wind against the hull. Flying in an aircraft is one thing—one expects the engines to be only some of a handful of things that will affect its movement. Gravity, wind, and the unfortunate bird or so are others. In space far enough removed from the pull of a celestial body, nothing typically pushes or stops you except yourself—you are literally and metaphorically the master of your ship, the commander of your soul's survival. Dealing with something unseen audibly rattling and tossing the metal can housing said soul, in a place normally without sound, pull, or push, would harrow even the best of pilots. The forces too, depending on how long he stayed in the fray, still carried enough of the sun's heat to slow-cook him. His palms were starting to sweat for both reasons.

Meran *hated* sweat. But it didn't matter. Not anymore. He was about to get an answer. Never mind the handkerchief in his suit pocket; he could barely stay in his seat. And never mind the alarms, the broken commands buzzing from his headphones, any reasoned warnings being whispered into his heart. He would *make* them tell him why. He would tell *them*—he would make them understand—his family hadn't deserved to die.

Just as he crested the farthest reaches of the wave, his hull creaking, his skin peeling from the heat, his ship no more than an ant to the hooves of the Beasts, Meran's head smacked into the side of his headrest.

When his eyes opened, the internal clock had progressed by fifteen standard minutes and eleven seconds. The sky around him was gray, blurred. His cockpit hatch hissed as it depressurized, then rose. There were handprints on the glass, one right and one left, both ashen gray. Then a medical team climbed aboard.

Oh no.

They each took an arm and began to lift him from his seat as a stretcher was raised to their level. He was back in the hangar.

This can't—no!

Vitals were checked, bandages unrolled, lights passed over his eyes. "Lieutenant Meran, please state your location. Count my raised fingers. Do you know who I am?"

You are not the one I was supposed to see!

The next few days slurred together.

No one understood why he had entered the storm, jeopardized the safety of the entire squadron. Did he not realize he had nearly died, that his plasma coils had inverted, taking on the storm's energy rather than expelling the engines' own waste, and he had been seconds away from total combustion? It was still unclear how he had made it out of the storm intact.

Meran was at first speechless, but told the council everything, forcing himself to explain the legends (even if they should have known them themselves). He had seen the chariots! He had! Given his record, his dedication, his skill, why shouldn't he be believed? Wasn't this a new frontier of exploration for Command? He tried to point out the gods in his ship's recovered footage, but it was as if he was grasping at smoke. He could find no hint of wheel, Beast, or spear —only his own fallen face staring back at him in the screen. They kept asking where the gods were. He was the one who was convinced he would speak to them; did he not get his wish? Did they not say anything to him, after all he'd said of them? Meran could not answer. His chest rang hollow with every quiver of his hearts.

Colonel Lae's sympathy was reaching its limits. She tapped her pen, rose, and humbly requested that Meran be put on monitored medical leave, not interrogated here and now. There were murmurs of a court marshal. Then, before Meran could even protest, he was whisked to the off-base transports, given his pay, and had his notebook sequestered for "review". When he arrived at his shrine, he was told to expect a call if he were to return to duty. He would not need to be troubled to call them first.

His adoptive parents were glad to see him, but mortified at his report. Everyone he told was. He grew to anticipate the shift in their eyes when relief faded into softened, but immutable concern.

He had done everything. And yet, somehow, it was smoke.

For the next two months he kept his eyes on the ground, seeing more sandals than faces, but dismissing both all the same. He kept himself occupied, daring not to think, staring off numbly when the hours came to pray. Only in the rare moments when his mother or cousin would come bearing food and take the broom or sponge from his hands did he sit still.

My offering was not pleasing to them. "Its odor was foul when burned, the lowest cut from among the gifts of the people," he recalled of the ancient texts. *I am the only one worshiping you among that entire fleet. There was no better gift I could have given. For what hidden sin do you turn your nose up at me? For what false justice did you make my parents die?*

At his family's insistence, one day, he went to rest under a shady tree a few yards from the shrine's entrance. He turned a fruit from the garden over in his hands. Sunlight danced across its surface, white rippling against deep purple, like foam over ocean waves.

Meran's stomach rumbled. He couldn't remember breakfast that morning, or dinner the night before. But he could not eat the fruit. He had forgotten to perform the ceremonial washings and prayers to be said before meals, and sweat from his hands was coating the rind. He would need to find a fountain and offer his thanksgiving. He couldn't bring himself to. He was not sure anyone would be there to hear it.

Some footsteps crunched along the path ahead. Meran's eyes followed the sound. Coming toward him was a woman with short hair, her glasses glinting in the light.

Her. He rose, silent.

"Lieutenant Meran," the statistics officer hailed him. His stomach churned. He couldn't bring himself to meet her eyes, but if he had, he would have been mildly...concerned by how disheveled she looked.

She sighed, slowly, gripping the strap of a rather full bag slung over her shoulder.

Meran lowered his head. The gesture turned into a bow, then near prostration.

"Lieutenant, what are you doing?"

"I am sorry," he choked. The officer flinched back. "You have been made to bring my belongings out this far. I have inconvenienced you with my failure."

"Your hypothesis is false. Please, rise."

Meran froze.

"I came here to speak with you."

His pulse thundered in his ears. "I am not discharged?"

The officer glanced away, out at the rippling grass. "The business is my own. And yours."

He was staring intently at her feet. At this, he realized she wasn't in standard issue boots, but in civilian shoes.

"I...would think you would still be running computations at this hour."

"I am on leave," she replied in a low voice.

It took a few moments to process this before he could climb back to his feet. The officer shifted, fidgeting.

"I saw your god," she said.

Meran was nearly sent back to the ground. The officer wouldn't look at him, and took his shock as room to continue talking.

"It was not possible on mathematical, epistemological, or even purely logical grounds," she rambled. "I cannot quantify the events even after the fact. My reports are useless, indecipherable—full of data points, but no lines to connect them. I have become completely ineffective at my own profession. Our superiors are not—"

"Tell me."

The officer stared; Meran trembled. It was only now he remembered her name—Ver'a cleared her throat.

"Your ship disappeared into the plasma storm—a storm of intensity beyond all previous records. It was approximately 3.11 minutes before it hit the *Rael* and we began to take on plasma as you did. The engineers do not understand how such a possibility was missed in the design. Yet I did not notice our state until the captain wrenched me from my station. It was then I realized. It was then I...prayed.

"I do not know why I did it. It was...illogical. I had no recourse remaining, and I reached out. I asked, if your gods were truly out there, that they would spare us, and spare you, whether it was we or you that must have angered them and brought this upon ourselves. And then I saw it. Him. I am still not certain. He was staring at me from beyond the porthole glass. He was like a child of Faria, and yet seemingly made of flame. He reached for my hand. I concluded that, as this was impossible, we had already overloaded, and my brain was passing through its final ejections of neurotransmitters before my consciousness dissipated. Thus there was no danger in returning the gesture, merely out of scientific curiosity. My hand passed through the hull, as though the bulkheads possessed the properties of water. I did not implode as I stepped out onto the starboard wing.

"I could not record his body temperature as the appropriate instruments remained onboard behind me, but I...felt only the need to walk toward this being. I still cannot describe his face distinctly enough for Command. But it was beauty."

"Not beautiful?"

Ver'a shook her head, brow furrowed. "It was the concept itself, not its imitation. It was what I had always seen in my calculations— reason, perfectly arrayed—but beyond what I could comprehend or touch. Yet he touched me, and took my hand in his own. His footprints are still on the wing of the *Rael*. Command cannot remove them. I have told them what I have experienced, but they do not understand. I was kept under observation for weeks—forgive me. I will continue.

"I was buffeted by the winds but felt no pain." She rolled up a sleeve to show fading burn scars from the storm. "Yet as I stared into his face, I gradually could not help but think of you, you who had so foretold this Being did exist. I approximated you were 86% likely to be unconscious, your engines 67.4% likely closer to overload than ours at that exact time sequence. Your unconsciousness, if unresolved within the next 27 seconds, would secure a 97.3% probability of fatality. As inefficient and irrational as I, on average, found you to be, I feared for you. For when I prayed, I had come to understand—you hoped in the unknown for prosperity. For understanding. For... purpose. As did I. We were not so different. Despite your arrogance, you never found our data to contradict that hope, only enhance the heights of reason. I could not leave you there to perish. Neither could your god.

"He took me to you, in the storm. My hands had taken on his own's glow, but were not consumed by his fire. By my count you had microseconds remaining, and—I do not say this to manipulate thanks from you—I pushed you, and without an opposite force from your engines, as you had stopped, well, you proceeded out from the storm. My physical did not qualify me for such a task but it nevertheless occurred."

She glanced up at Meran, apparently for reassurance, but he said nothing. His fists were tightening. She cleared her throat again.

"When your engines cooled, I was led back to the *Rael*. It was as though no time had passed. The child sat me down and touched my console, and its status lights returned to green. One by one, so did the others. The engines began to cool. I looked up, and the child was gone, without a word, but I have never before felt such...peace.

"We collected you and returned to base. Most of the crew were given leave. But Lieutenant, the *data* we collected. Our systems should barely have retained a byte, but our understanding of plasma dynamics has leapt forward a hundred—no, two hundred years by this experience. The applications to medicine alone are unimaginable. We should have genetic diseases cured within the next decade! It—it is *beautiful*, Meran!"

Meran still did not reply. Ver'a, in her joy, suddenly grew quiet. "Do you not think so?"

The lieutenant turned away. Years, decades even of dedication, and this—*this* was his answer? An arrogant unbeliever, one who sneered at the mere suggestion of metaphysics, was the one to not only *see*, but *walk* with a god? A god unseen for centuries, despite even longer begging that once, just once, his face would be seen among them, his heart would turn back toward his sinful people, his breath would give them life and *understanding* and—

A hand came to rest on his back. "You are crying."

—comfort.

Meran sank to his knees, inconsolable. It would naturally be "the opinion of the statistics office" that he was emotionally disturbed, wholly unfit for duty. But, marvel of marvels, Ver'a did not leave him as he sobbed. Only sat by him, in the dust, and after a while handed him a peeled section of his fruit, long forgotten nearby.

She hesitated for a moment, but finally spoke. "It is reasonable for you to return inside. I hoped for your analysis, but I have troubled you enough. I understand shrines do not permit nonbelievers on their grounds for concern of defilement."

He would not have done the same for her, he thought, watching the sunlight dance around the fruit's beaded flesh. He would not have had the same preoccupation. If he were with his god, with her ship about to burst, it would have seemed the logical conclusion to the life of one who had worshipped logic itself: *she* was unworthy. *He*, faithful, would have been proven right. He would have saved her, but while so caught up in his worship that he would have left its object behind, staring after him in space.

That was never worship to begin with.

Meran took the fruit. He looked at her, his eyes raw.

"Please. Come with me," he said, then swallowed hard. "The shrine is open to all who earnestly seek truth."

Ver'a's eyes took on that same sunlight.

They walked together toward the gates, discoursing of the mission even as they entered.

Story 11

What Sustains Us

E.P. Fuselier

The first story I ever wrote was stolen from the bus stop. Someone could say it was my fault because I had left it there, but how much can you blame a snotty pre-teen? I only realized it was missing when I got to school that day, tearing through my backpack, hoping, praying I hadn't left it on the bus. No one could read that story. Not the other kids, not the bus driver, not even my teacher—no one. It *had* started off as a school assignment, but once I had the whole thing out on paper, stapled with the sheets all uneven, I realized I couldn't turn it in. I didn't even know why at first. I just shoved it in a drawer and turned in some piece of crap I wrote the morning it was due, which had earned me a measly C plus. But that first story, that one stayed in my drawer like Poe's telltale heart. (I wouldn't understand that reference for a few years, but when I finally read that story, I understood his fear.)

And like Poe's character, I found I couldn't leave it in its hiding place. What if my mom was cleaning my room and found it? What if she read it? The horror of that was too much for me to risk. So to school with me it came, a hidden passenger whose only purpose was to stay secret. It went back and forth for a few days with me, my backpack roughing it up as if welcoming it into a gang. (Maybe my mom was right back then about my dad letting me watch too many mob movies.)

Then one day at the bus stop, with the dew glistening on the overgrown grass in front of the tall house on the corner where we waited for the bus, the small gaggle of us forcing back yawns, Jenny Lejune got to talking about trading snacks. She had those cardboard animal crackers, and while I wasn't too fond of them either, I also wasn't a fool, even at twelve years old. The Fruit by the Foot wasn't too steep a price to pay considering Bud Elliot gave me a dirty look when Jenny passed up his mini Chips Ahoy cookies.

But in digging through my backpack to pay the beautiful girl with braids down her back, I must have somehow displaced the story from its cave of secrets. All day I could only think about where it had gone, who had gotten a hold of it, who was *reading* it. I was unable to banish the tightness gripping my chest and even though I knew I was surly with my teachers and short with my friends, I couldn't seem to help it. Could Bud Elliot have picked it up? Was he even now snickering to his little buddies, mocking my spies and assassins? I glanced back at him where he sat at the back of the bus, but while he was being rambunctious and showy, his attention wasn't focused on me.

I turned toward the front, and sat up on my knees as we started to creep toward our stop. If I had left it there, I needed to be the first one out and grab it before anyone could see it. Straining, I peered through the windows. There was the curved sidewalk, backed by the dilapidated two story house that stood on the corner lot. And stooping toward the sidewalk was an old man, reaching toward something white and rectangular on the ground.

Alarm shot through my stomach, making me feel sick and shaky.

No, no, no.

Not old man Sythe. I could tell it was him because that was his house and no one else dressed like him. He always wore suspenders and high waisted pants, like he had walked straight out of another century. The man was an aloof loner, but had been here so long that his seeming permanence was the only reason anyone knew who he was. If he took it, getting it back would be impossible.

I stood bolt upright as the brakes of the bus squealed out. If I could run out there and explain it was mine, I could have it back before he could flip over the first page. I squirmed in anticipation, staring out the window as the bus slowly rolled to a stop. Old Man Sythe straightened, examining my story in his hands, then he looked up at the bus. He seemed to peer inside, as if he were searching or deliberating, and I felt as if I somehow wasn't safe, as if he was looking for me. I should have moved, hopped off the bus before everyone so I could launch myself onto the sidewalk and snatch the story back. But instead, I remained rooted, lurching forward into the seat in front of me as the bus stopped fully. The other departing kids crowded the aisle, so I waited behind them in frustration, and was only released at the end of the line.

Finally I jumped off onto the curb, but the sidewalk was empty. No Sythe, no story. I spun toward the house and could see the back of the old man ambling up his front steps. Just barely, I could make out the papers in his hand. I thought about calling out, but there was something about that house that stopped me. It wasn't painted black and kids didn't go missing after ding-dong ditching or any weird neighborhood stories like that. With peeling paint and a few rotting exterior panels, there wasn't anything big that made it feel *off*, and it certainly wasn't the only house on our street that was unkempt, but it had presence. It wasn't anything I could pinpoint. I always thought it was older than the rest of the houses around it, with different architecture from the others, and it didn't seem to like me.

I certainly didn't want to even step foot in the yard, not even to retrieve my story. I watched as Sythe disappeared into his house, my chest rising in quick breaths. My story was gone, and I had just stood there.

.   .   .

After hours of stewing in my room, I had formulated a plan. My dad had stayed late for work (again) and my mom, all angry and silent, had sent me to bed. I didn't go to sleep, but instead concocted my brilliant infiltration. Well, the first hour was actually spent convincing myself to even retrieve the story.

I stared at the old house across the street, lit by the sun's dying light, although the light wasn't doing it any favors. What used to be garden beds were overgrown, the mail box was slightly askew and a window shutter was hanging crooked. It was usually easy to ignore, but that evening, it was the proverbial house on the hill (even if the hill was a small mound that raised the house a few feet of elevation). It had a deep yard, further set into the lot than most of the houses on our street. The distance wasn't far, just an easy walk across the street and then maybe crawling across the lawn to ensure I wouldn't be seen, but from the vantage point of my room on the second story, it seemed like I was looking at a battlefield. The overgrown bushes and thick grass were obstacles I'd have to crawl around. Then I'd have to climb the steps of the porch, avoiding any creaking of old boards, and sneak on the wraparound porch to the back door. From there I'd have to force my way in, maybe break a window, which was risky, but sitting here all these hours doing nothing had convinced me that I needed that story back.

I had tried to rationalize myself out of this insane quest. It wasn't that important. Who cared if old man Sythe read my story? He probably wouldn't know who I was, even though my name was on it. It was just a dumb story, but unfortunately it was so dumb that I didn't want anyone to put their eyes on it. The concept was too embarrassing to bear. So despite all of these solid reasons, I made up my mind to get it back because the buzzing knot in my chest wouldn't listen. Even if it was stupid, I was going to leave the safety of my house, cross the street, traverse the yard, and break into the house. It was the only way to get away from this gut twisting feeling. Intimidating house or no, stupid idea or not, I was going to get that story back.

I'd have to wait until my dad came home before I snuck out, which was fine; the later this happened, the safer I would feel. I put on all black, making sure to turn my long sleeve shirt inside out to hide the Nike swoosh. It was a small detail, but the spies I had written about in my story wouldn't have made any slip ups like that.

It was a little before midnight when my dad came home. I had to wait a good while longer for my parents to argue themselves out. Normally, I'd press my pillow onto my ears so that I didn't have to listen, but this time, I needed to know when they went to bed. So I had to bear through their angry voices sounding up through the floor of my room, but finally the house was quiet, dark and locked up, and my clock read 1:15.

I rubbed my eyes. Being tired tomorrow was fine. I crept down the stairs, and, unlocking the backdoor, slipped out into the night with my heart pounding.

A rumble sounded in the distance, and I glanced up at the sky. Clouds covered any light from the moon and stars, and wind threatened to blow my hoodie off. Rain, now? After all this time I had waited? It had held off this long, and so I decided to risk it. The route I had mapped out in my head was somehow easier to journey than the hours I had spent planning it. I sped across the street, my form low as if that would keep someone from spotting me. I reached the yard and dropped to my stomach just as a flash of lightning lit up the sky. Hold off just a little longer.

I army crawled across the grass and hunched behind the bushes. The house loomed in front of me. Maybe the dusk light had been doing something for it, because in the darkness, it seemed much more like a haunted house, the darkness lending it a sense of mystery and danger. I almost turned back then, but a drop of rain seeped into the arm of my sweatshirt. Better get in and out before the storm hit in earnest. So I took a deep breath and forced myself to climb the steps of the porch. I peered into a window. It was dark inside, but I could make out vague shapes, tall, thin, and rectangular.

Rain began to fall, splattering on the roof and the plants, a variety of thousands of splatters and splunks. I had gotten under cover just in time. But going home—I'd just have to run as fast as I could. And if the story got wet and was destroyed, all the better. My clothes would be soaked when I got home, but I could change once there.

I tried the backdoor and found it unlocked. Okay, luck was on my side. I eased it open slowly, trying to ward against any alerting squeaks. It protested a bit, but allowed me to enter relatively silently. I closed it behind me and turned to face the darkened house. Putting my hand over my flashlight, I flicked it on and then allowed only a sliver of light to escape.

Stacks of books took up every space I could see. They made up walls of their own, giving the room a claustrophobic feeling. How was I going to find it in this mess? Maybe I should check the front of the house. It would make sense for him to drop it there after finding it on the sidewalk. I went in the direction I guessed would lead me to the front. I glanced at the stacks as I passed them, hoping to see leaves of paper, but only dust and odd objects occupied their surfaces.

I entered what should have been the kitchen, but the books taking up most of the counter space, stacked on the stove, would prevent it from being functional. Maybe there was a trash can in here. Maybe he hadn't read it at all but instead thought it was just garbage. But despite finding the can against the wall, my story wasn't in there. I quickly continued on through the house and found a room with what looked like the front door. A small desk was pressed against the wall and covered in papers. The window in front of the desk showed me a flash of lightning and thick sheets of rain. That was a problem for later. I started rifling through the papers, thinking it would most likely be on top, but I had to be thorough.

Someone grabbed me by the shoulder and spun me around. I screamed as sheer terror ripped through my veins and my roving flashlight revealed the leering face of old man Sythe.

"Quiet! Quiet! Quiet!" he roared over my screams. "Hush, boy!"

"I'm sorry!" I blubbered, not lowering my volume in the least, instead trying to yell over him. "I didn't mean to—" He yanked me to the side as he began walking down the hallway. "I don't want to get in trouble, please!"

"Be quiet!" he growled. His tight grip forced me along until we came to a room where he flipped on the light. We were in a study with a large old fashioned desk on one side—books once again stacked on most of the open space—and bookshelves lining every wall. A large, arched window rose almost to the top of the ceiling. Outside, torrents of rain pounded the glass and the street lights lit up a scene of violence. Even if I bolted out of here and made it to the back door, the wind looked like it was dragging the trees through the ringer. I felt like I was trapped on an island, with trees made out of books and a maniac man who ran it all.

Old Man Sythe placed me in the center of the room as if I were on trial and let go, stepping away to stand by the desk. I swallowed thickly, my heart threatening to leap out of my chest.

"I'm sor—"

"What's your name?" he interrupted.

"D-Drew."

"Drew." He stared at me for a moment. "I'm Sythe. You live across the street? In the house with the basketball goal and the blue door?"

I nodded, terrified he'd call my parents or the police.

But he didn't say anything, just stared at me, like he was searching me, or studying me. Finally, after a tortuous, interminable few seconds, he spoke. "You came here for this?" From the desk, he picked up my story, now more crumpled than ever before.

"Yeah, I—I need it for school."

He stared at it then up at me, then gruffly said, "You could have just knocked on the door."

I swallowed. "I—I just really needed it back." I searched for words, but I was too busy fighting back tears.

He peered at me scrupulously, and I looked down.

"I didn't want you to read it," I said.

"Why? It's a good story."

I snapped my head up. "You read—"

"There's nothing too embarrassing in there."

I looked down again, unable to watch him search through it. I heard the shuffling of paper but couldn't bring myself to look up.

Shff, shff, shff went the sheets.

"The family's pretty happy," Sythe observed gruffly.

I stared at my shoe trying to see how far I could dig into the rug and shrugged. "Yeah."

"A family of spies who go on this pretty intense adventure together." Another flip of a page. "And they don't fight at all. That's pretty impressive."

I twisted my lips to the side. "Well, I just thought if they're going to be fighting bad guys, they could, you know, at least not be fighting with each other."

We stood in silence for a long moment, him flipping the pages until it sounded like he flopped it on the desk.

"Would you like to know a secret?" he asked.

I looked up with a frown, but didn't say anything.

He nodded thoughtfully, looked me in the eyes, and said quite plainly, "I am immortal."

My frown deepened to one of skepticism, and he laughed. "I know, an impossibility. But it's true. As long as I have stories to read, I can live on indefinitely. That's why I took your story there." He pointed to where it lay on the desk. "I can read my old favorites and they'll keep me going, and as you see," he gestured to the walls around us, "my house is full of them. But even if I keep on living, I still feel old. My bones hurt, my chest aches, my joints creak. It's only the fresh stuff that makes me *feel* young again. And that, that was some good stuff." He pointed at my stack of paper again.

I narrowed my eyes. "Are you lying?" I didn't need an adult to lie to me to make me feel better, but this would be a really weird lie and I didn't see how it was supposed to cheer me up. Why make it up?

But it couldn't be real. That would be crazy.

"I'm not," he said easily. "But I can see how it's difficult to believe."

I folded my arms across my chest. "So what happens if you read a bad story?"

He smiled. "A logical question. If it's just a poorly written story —" He threw up his hands in a shrug. "Doesn't really do anything to me. Doesn't sustain my life, but it doesn't hurt me. Or it might give me only a little bit of life, an inconsequential amount."

"Can a story hurt you?" I asked, wary and skeptical. But I was also fascinated. I didn't really believe him, but it was too interesting to not at least ask questions and poke at his tall tale.

"They can. I don't know if you've encountered these kinds of stories—I hope not—but it's those kinds that when you finish it, your stomach is in a kind of knotted mess, leaving you with a sense of unease or ickiness. It's the kind that makes you feel like it's not worth continuing on tomorrow, the kind where the hero disappoints you, or it's not worth it to take another step. Those kinds of stories, those rob me of some of my life."

"So, like, Where the Red Fern Grows. We had to read that for school, and it was pretty sad."

"I don't mean sad stories. I mean the despairing ones. Where the Red Fern Grows...I can see how a kid like you might not jive with it, but someone else, it might mean something to them."

I thought about the sense of shock that had struck me when I witnessed Jenny Lejune crying on the bus as she flipped through the last few pages of the book. When we discussed it in class, she had spoken about it with a kind of awe or something.

"OK, but I still don't understand what you mean by a despairing story."

He nodded. "Yeah, I think books for kids your age generally hit the mark when it comes to the good kind of spirit I'm talking about. It's when you get to be a teenager, and worse when you're an adult." He shook his head. "It's like they think we don't know the world is a depressing place and need to be reminded of it."

"You're not really selling the whole growing up thing. And if you don't like it so much, why do you want to keep extending it?"

"Just because there's bad things in the world or even bad things happening to oneself, that's not the same as life not being worth continuing on."

"So you just…read stories all day? Making sure they're only good ones?" It sounded super boring. What was the point?

"It's what I do with a lot of my time, yes." He paused and took a turn around the room, examining his books. I glanced at their spines, wondering if what he was saying could really be true. There were all different kinds of books, tall, short, thick, thin, old ones with their bindings falling off and new ones with shiny dust jackets. He was probably just a hoarder and had to come up with this tale to justify himself.

His pensive stroll finally brought him to the tall window where the rain beat against the panes furiously. I had a straight shot to the door, but then I would have to go out into that storm. When would it let up?

"To be honest," he finally said, "I might be a little afraid of living life without my stories within reach. I don't know how long I can go in between before I start to waste away. What if I don't get there in time?"

"You could always just carry books with you." That seemed pretty obvious to me.

He nodded, but his stare out into the black of the night was distant.

"And anyway," I said, "everyone else has to live without the guarantee that they're going to live forever. Seems kinda—" I wanted to say wimpy, but that seemed rude after this guy hadn't called the cops on me. Instead, I shrugged. "—I don't know. Like you're afraid."

He turned to me with a curious but unrelenting gaze. "Are you afraid?"

"No."

"No? It seems to me you're afraid of something."

I glared and folded my arms across my chest. "I snuck in here, didn't I?"

He chuckled lightly. "*Snuck* is debatable." He took a breath where I was about to argue, but he continued before I could. "But in my experience, someone is much more likely to do something reckless when they are fleeing from something even worse."

I bit my lip and stared past him, my turn to lock eyes with the darkness in the window.

"It's difficult when your parents don't get along."

"I came for the story!" I snapped, throwing my hands to the side. I expected him to get mad at my anger, like adults always did, as if they were the only one allowed to react that way.

But instead, he studied me for a long moment, then finally said, "I am unique in that I can live on stories, but I am not the only one who can be sustained by them." Again he gestured to my pages. "When you feel like you're in a dark time, like you're being swallowed up by the fear, by the what ifs, it's stories that can get you through. Read them. Write them. Even before they were extending my years supernaturally, they bolstered me."

I stared at my hands, pressing them together. Then quietly I said, "I don't think writing a story will keep my parents together. I don't even know why I wrote it. It just kinda came out."

"And yet you journeyed into my fortress to retrieve it. It seems you may have become the hero of your own tale."

I shook my head. "No, I just didn't want anyone to see—" I paused, trying to work around the words. "My story is so kid-ish. All the cool books have the parents dying and the kids on their own who do something really clever to save the day. This was just cheesy. I came here cuz I was embarrassed of anyone reading it."

He was silent as he nodded. "Well, you may not believe me, but when I read it, it gave me a surge of vigor, a thing I have not felt in a long time." He looked up at his chandelier. "It makes me wonder how long I've stayed cooped up in here, content with an extended life of stagnation. I've read stories that had much better technical writing, but a lot of them are those depressing adult books I talked about. This one had *life*."

"Well," I said, pressing my shoe into that same spot on the rug, "if you like it that much, you can keep it."

"That would mean a great deal to me. In return, I have a gift for you." He crossed the room and from a spot in the corner, he pulled out a thin book. Turning back to me, he walked the few steps that separated us and handed it to me. "I think this one will resonate with you."

I took it from him and looked at the cover. It was an orange hard-back book with a giant yellow sun in the center, the words *The Alchemist,* and at the bottom, *Paolo Coelho.* I had never heard of it before, but I wasn't going to reject it. "Thanks," I mumbled.

He looked up at the window and exclaimed with a smack of his lips, "Ah! It seems the worst of the storm has passed. I can send you home with an umbrella without fear of you being blown away."

He walked me to his front door which would give me the more direct route to my house. I remained silent as I walked on his worn rugs, the wooden floorboards creaking lightly under my feet. My mind was full of his words. I wasn't sure what to make of most of them, but they had substance, had something that made me want to chew on them.

He unlocked the front door and grabbed an umbrella from a brass stand. We both stepped out onto the porch where he popped open the umbrella and handed it to me.

I took it, and feeling embarrassed, said, "Thanks for not calling the cops on me. And you know...the book." And for his words about stories, and his lie about immortality. I could now recognize it was a nice way to ease my anxiety. But I wasn't going to call him out on that. It was nice to have this inside joke to hold onto without bursting the illusion, a little story of his I could carry with me in my memory.

"I find I must thank you," he said. "This was an unexpected plea-sure for a grumpy old man set in his ways. It's been a long time since I've been blindsided by the gumption of youth."

I hefted the umbrella, readying myself to go out into the now drizzling rain.

"If you could find some time to bring it back," he said, pointing to the umbrella, "don't be afraid to knock on my door. And I wouldn't mind hearing more about this family of spies you've created."

I nodded but didn't have any words. Then I turned and climbed down the steps into the rain.

* * *

I climbed those steps many times over the years, spent a lot of time on that porch, swapping stories with old man Sythe, him explaining *The Alchemist*—the book that saved my life—or any other book I happened to be reading. We talked in the freezing cold, in pollen laden days, in the unbearable heat, the crunching, swirling leaves. But after I had graduated high school, those visits became less and less frequent.

I found myself treading up the stairs again today. No peeling paint, but instead they were fresh, bordered by a diverse, packed, but cultivated garden bed.

"Drew Casey!" came Sythe's roaring voice from the porch. "How dare you kill off my favorite character!"

I laughed lightly, climbing up the last few steps onto the porch. He sat in his regular rocking chair, puffing out a pipe, a stack of books on one table next to him, and another table spread with a coffee cup and various loose papers. A carafe stood at the ready for whatever guests might stumble onto his porch, partnered with a pitcher of lemonade for the kids who frequented his yard these days. Sythe looked as he ever did, a small smile at his lips, his skin wrinkled but not any more weathered than I was used to. It felt like I was fifteen again.

"Are you kidding me?" I said as I walked across the porch. "You were the one who lectured me about how *The Bridge to Terabithia* was a good book."

"That doesn't mean you just just kill off characters willy-nilly."

I sat in a chair opposite him. "It wasn't willy-nilly at all. You're just getting too sentimental in your old age."

"I am not." He leaned forward toward the carafe, and in a grumble asked, "You want some coffee?"

"Always." I could blame my healthy coffee addiction on the many porch visits we'd had over the years. The deadlines for high school and college and then later for my editor late into the night had only made it worse.

He took the carafe and poured into a waiting cup. "You knew I liked Molly. I think you owe me a favor for killing her off." I waited with a smile as he passed the cup to me, black with no sugar. "When are you ever going to get back to that spy family?"

I grinned and took a sip. "Not sentimental?"

"It was a great story!"

"No it wasn't. It was just something I needed to write at the time. It served its purpose."

He glared at me good-naturedly. "That's a callous way to treat a story, forgotten and never able to be shared with the rest of the world."

"I disagree," I said, putting my cup on the table next to me. "Some stories we just need to write for ourselves. I was a scared twelve year old kid who needed to process the fact that his parents were splitting up. I appreciate it for what it did for me, but—" I shook my head with a light laugh. "—I don't hold your opinion that it was actually *good*."

"I don't care if you do have a best seller out there. If you'd read as many books as I have, you'd understand how to treasure a good story, even if it is a little amateurish."

I picked up my cup again and studied him as he launched into a synopsis of the story one of the neighborhood kids had written for him. He had some criticisms, but his eyes shone as he described its halting, awkward but ambitious plot. Despite what he said, I knew he had a blind spot when it came to the stories from kids. Still, it was good to see the tradition of leaving tales for Old Man Sythe in the free library in his front yard in exchange for a prize was going strong. He looked the same as he had when I had broken into his house all those years ago, no more wizened or worn than my memory of him. Indeed, today he had a liveliness, a certain mischievous pull on his lips that wasn't there the night I met him.

"You look good," I said after a while.

He nodded. "Yeah, I got a good story from this little girl last week." He shook his head in amazement, as if he were savoring a delicious bite of food. "It had plants that would only grow when sung to. It had me performing for my gardenias."

I watched him for a few seconds. "Sythe, can I ask you something?"

He tilted his head with a chiding look, as if to say I didn't need to ask.

"The whole story of you being immortal," I continued, "that's bullshit, right? You've just got good genes or have some crazy good health regimen, right?" He had always maintained through the years his tale of books sustaining him, but surely now that I was an adult, he'd come clean. I was long past the point of needing to be placated.

He took a long pull of his pipe and let the smoke rise in a beautiful ring toward the white washed shiplap ceiling. "Drew, you should know the best part about a good story is that they're true." He looked out past me, to his yard, the neighborhood, to the greater world and sighed deeply. "At least true in the sense that matters."

Acknowledgments

Publishing a short story collection is no easy feat and takes work from far more folks than just our authors and editors. It is a difficult thing to properly thank all those who have contributed to this collection, even in a small way, but here we hope to be as encompassing as we can. Chief amongst those persons who had a hand in this collection's creation is the Author of all life, God, who created us as curious and creative creatures. In Jesus' sacrifice we may find the greatest source of Hope, from which all other hope stems. For the gifts of the ability to participate in subcreation and the talents of our authors, we thank you.

To Catherine Broussard, who founded Inkwells & Anvils along with E.P. "Little" Fuselier, Grace "Hopkins" Malinee, Tyler Carlos, Rob, Paige Guerra, Lauren, and Kelly. Without Catherine's efforts in leading the community and her diligence in making it a home for so many wandering writers, this book would not be. Somehow, despite all the work she does in her ministry and maintaining a social life, she finds the time to encourage all of us. Catherine, thank you!

Next we would like to thank all of our editors and judges. To the judging team: E.P. Fuselier, Kelly Gross, Ben Stapleton, Robert M. Hart, and Tyler Carlos, we thank you all for your diligence in reading every submitted work and making the hard decisions over which of the stories would be included. We had Grace Malinee, E. P. Fuselier, and Ben Stapleton who worked with some of our authors to chisel these stories into publication shape. Grace's skill with plotting is outdone only by her tenacity, E. P.'s discerning eye for pacing is matched only by her patience, and Ben's penchant for voice is outshone only by his eccentricity. We also thank Paige Guerra and E. P. once again for their line editing contributions.

We also want to thank every author who submitted a short story for our consideration. While not every author was published, we hope that those authors who were not will be included in a future collection. Most especially we thank those contributors who are published in this collection and who have not already been thanked (in order of their appearance): S.J. Delacosta, Caspar, Madeline Shepley, Augustin Cavalier, Gwendalina K.K. Buller, and Elizabeth Ruda. For your efforts in expressing Hope through the written word, we thank you.

Finally, each of our contributors has a short list of collaborators, co-conspirators, and comrades to whom they would like to especially express gratitude. In no particular order these are St Dymphna & St Gerebran (both for their prayers and inspiration), Caspar's wife, the Wordsmiths, Whitney, Carah, Evan, Josh, Alan, Lee, S.J. Delacosta, Elizabeth, Augustin's family, Josh, S.J. Delacosta's family & friends, Mrs Stanley, Clara, Rachael, Ben, Madeline, Nick, Miles, Dominic Perry, Anna, Danuta, Leszek, Iwo, Fr Donald Siple, L.L. Lee, and Gabe. To any others who were not named here but helped shape all of our author's beautiful stories, we give our sincerest thanks.

Last and not least we would like to thank you, dear reader, for your willingness to read our stories, to breathe in what these wonderful authors have made, and for your hope despite the storms. We thank you.

- The Inkwells & Anvils Anthology Team

Meet Our Authors

In order of appearance

E. P. Fuselier is one of the founders of Inkwells & Anvils, a journey which started when she followed the Holy Spirit's prompting to grow in her craft of writing alongside other Catholic authors. She loves writing fantasy but enjoys reading all sorts of genres—fantasy, sci-fi, historical non-fiction, biographies. While she hates cliches, she still says her favorite authors are J.R.R. Tolkien, C.S. Lewis, and Jane Austen.

S.J. Delacosta is an aspiring novelist with a passion for storytelling through the lens of speculative fiction, viewing it as a compelling vehicle through which to reflect upon the human condition. A jack of many trades, Delacosta enjoys spending time outdoors hiking, kayaking, and climbing the occasional boulder.

Caspar wrote the story that has his name under it. For further incriminating information, make sure to complete his companion quest and find all five of the red-legged cormorants hidden throughout the stage.

Grace F. Hopkins is an editor, writer, and co-founder of Inkwells & Anvils. Her short fiction has appeared most recently in "Mysterion" and "Horrorsmith" magazines. She flavors her fiction with both the eldritch & the transcendental and Tweets about writing

@graceswritesalt. She is also a proud member of the Catholic Artist Network of St. Louis.

BEN STAPLETON primarily writes science fiction and fantasy. He has yet to publish any novels, though he claims to be working on some. You can find his short fiction in Inkwells & Anvils' other collections. By day he sunlights as an electrical engineer and by night can be found painting miniatures, reading, or writing. Otherwise you can find him (or don't, as he likes the solitude) hiking or hunting in the back woods of Pennsylvania.

MADELINE SHEPLEY is a planetarium director and physics & astronomy professor who moonlights as a faith-inspired sci-fi author in her spare time. She is a Hoosier, bred and educated, where she first developed a passionate love of astronomy, reading, and writing. When not delving into stories or stargazing, you might find her podcasting, cheering on her favorite sports teams, or plotting her next international excursion. You can find other published short stories of hers in the Dawn of Legend Fiction and There'll Be Scary Ghost Stories anthologies.

AUGUSTIN CAVALIER writes words, code, and (on rare occasion) music. He is also capable of reading, and when doing so, his interests are many and varied but often have a philosophical bent. Besides writing and reading, he can regularly be heard singing and chanting in various choirs and scholas, as well as arguing animatedly about one thing or another, though hopefully not both at the same time.

CATHERINE BROUSSARD works full time in youth ministry but makes time for more hobbies and interests than you'd think is reasonable. A co-founder of Inkwells & Anvils, Catherine pours her community building (and managing) skills into the I&A Discord server daily— while still writing her own epic fantasy & theological works on the side. Recently married, Catherine enjoys spending time with her husband, playing TTRPGs, and occasionally picking up her own paintbrush again. Follow her endeavors on X & Instagram: @acatholicgeek

PAIGE GUERRA is a proud co-founder of Inkwells & Anvils. She started work on her first novel in 2020, but has been writing stories since she could type fast enough to keep up with her ideas. While working as a registered nurse all over the United States, she balances critiquing her fellow WordSmiths' writing with her own projects that span topics such as dystopian horror, sci-fi adventure, writing craft, and motorsports journalism. You can find more of her short fiction published with Short Fiction Break and Uncharted Magazine. Or, for something more chaotic, you can follow her passionate fandom of all things Spider-Man, Formula One, Broadway, and Disney on any social media.

GWENDALINA KLARA KAROLINA BULLER is a Catholic writer. She lives in a Polish countryside full of small houses, fields and picturesque meadows where wild animals come to visit from the nearby forest sometimes. When she's not writing, you might find her working on something else creative like music and acting, researching history or on a long walk, singing songs and admiring the beauty around. She aspires to become a bardess, go on a pilgrimage following footsteps of Celtic Saints and have a secret library one day.

ELIZABETH RUDA is an editor, author, and artist based in St. Louis, MO. With one foot in fantasy and the other in sci-fi, she works to bring the Church's truth, beauty, and goodness to an aching world. Her work can be found in the previous I&A anthology, There'll Be Scary Ghost Stories, as well as on the St. Louis Catholic Artist Network site and her personal LinkedIn.

About Inkwells & Anvils

Inkwells & Anvils is an online community that seeks to provide a home for Catholic storytellers who want to pursue the perfection of their craft and find freedom to explore the good, the true, and the beautiful in that same craft as a means of glorifying our Creator. We believe in art with all its teeth and acknowledge that, in the realm of Catholic storytelling, there is no "one size fits all" approach. We see our ability to co-create with our Lord through the gifts and talents he has bestowed upon us as just that: a gift that we seek not only to treasure but to protect and respect through the work that we do. We remember the words of one of our patron Saints, St. Francis de Sales, when he said, "Be who you are and be that well."

* * *

Also By Inkwells & Anvils:

There'll Be Scary Ghost Stories: An Inkwells & Anvils Anthology

* * *

Find out more & join Inkwells & Anvils:

Our Website: inkwellsandanvils.com

X & Instagram: @inkwellsanvils

* * *

Inkwells & Anvils is proud to remain free from generative AI-usage in any part of anything contained in our published works.